£7

Long Road to Iona
& other stories

Janet Walkinshaw

Published in 2014 by FeedARead.com Publishing – Arts Council funded.

A CIP catalogue record for this title is available from the British Library.

Cover design: fuzzyblue.

For Randolph

Contents

Lady in a Hat

Sally decided on the pink floaty frock. The length was just right, mid-knee, flattering without being grannyish. It would do nicely, with the white linen jacket that sat so neatly over her hips. It was a long time since she'd first worn these clothes, but Mother-of-the-Bride outfits never dated. She eased on the skin coloured tights, with a sheen to them, and examined her legs carefully. No horrible varicose veins yet, thank you Lord. The beige shoes with the two inch heel would be the most comfortable, for you never knew on a day like this how much walking or standing around would be needed. She had danced so often in these shoes (whatever became of all those wonderful men?) but she had cared for them and they still looked as good as new. Matching handbag. That was essential. It was easy to spoil the whole effect with the wrong accessories. The string of pinkish pearls flattered her skin and didn't pretend to be real. Real was so passé.

Just a smidgin of makeup, the lipstick the same shade as the frock. At her age less was more.

And then the hat. Ah yes, the hat. Creamy silk swathed the crown and lace the colour of candy floss frothed round the brim. It was unmistakably a special occasion, a once in a lifetime, a celebration hat, a nonsense hat. Some actors swore by the shoes, some by the wig. But she'd always believed in the hat. The hat was the way in to the soul of the character. She could hear her very first wardrobe mistress in Shaftesbury Avenue saying Get the hat right, dear, and everything else falls into place.

She turned slowly in front of the mirror, seeing herself from three angles. She looked the part to perfection.

The bus journey took just under an hour and a half. She noted that none of the people who alighted with her was carrying luggage. She walked slowly down the side street that led to the centre of town, and entered the railway station. She was the only one from the bus.

There were three women in the waiting room, surrounded by luggage, and two backpackers stretched out on the plastic benches, asleep. She settled down to wait.

The three women were chattering, with an occasional burst of laughter. Judging by the high spirits, they were at the start of a holiday. Sally hoped they were going somewhere warm and it would be everything they wished. She hoped that when they returned they would still be friends. Soon one of them glanced at her watch and they gathered themselves together and left.

A man with a briefcase came in and sat down and opened his newspaper. The backpackers were still asleep, the boy snuffling as if he had a cold.

Sally opened her handbag. Then she searched it. Then she scrabbled more loudly and more frantically. She began to whimper. She removed everything from the handbag and laid the contents out along the bench. Lipstick, handkerchief, comb, buspass, a train ticket, a folded piece of paper, pillbox.

'Oh my goodness,' she wailed, and turned the handbag upside down and shook it.

Always conscious of her audience, she was aware of the man watching her by now.

She seized the handkerchief, shook it out and wiped her eyes.

'Is anything wrong?' the man asked.

'I've lost my purse.'

'Caught in the lining.'

She shook the handbag upside down again so that he could see.

'I've lost it or left it at home or something and I've just arrived here and I'm supposed to get a taxi to a wedding it's being held in a hotel somewhere or other in the country I've just come in on the train and I don't know this place and I don't know what to do.'

The man had come over and was sitting beside her by now. She thrust the makeup and the train ticket back into her bag. The ticket was an old one and she didn't want him seeing the date on it.

He picked up the piece of paper and read it. It had the name of a hotel, which was purely imaginary.

He was looking at her hat, and half smiling.

'Can't you phone? Get someone to pick you up?'

'Yes. No. I don't know the number. It's my nephew's wedding, you see. The family are staying at a hotel, not that one, I don't know which one, and I don't even know the bride's surname. There's nobody to phone. Oh dear.'

Feel the reality of it in your gut, her old drama teacher had said. Right down to your liver and pancreas and spleen you *are* the person. She burst into tears.

'Look,' he said, reaching into his pocket. 'Let me give you some money for the taxi.'

'Oh no.'

'Yes, I insist.'

She wailed again.

'It's too good of you. I suppose I must. Oh, how stupid I am. But give me your address of course and as soon as I get home I'll put a cheque in the post to you. I only need enough for a taxi. About ten pounds they told me, my nephew said it would be, including the tip and another niece is going to put me up and then tomorrow someone will drive me home, but they couldn't fetch me today because...'

She stopped with a sob. The man had pulled out his wallet and was leafing through the notes in it. He took out a twenty pound note and handed it to her.

'It's all right,' he said. 'You don't have to pay it back. It's a rotten position to be in. Supposing it was my ...' He paused. She did so hope he had been going to say My Mother, but feared it was My Granny.

'No, no. I insist,' she said. 'Tell me your name.'

He took his business card from his wallet and handed it to her. She read it. Something senior on the engineering side of an aeronautical company.

'Oh,' she said. 'My husband was an engineer. He had a heart of gold.' This was nearly true. When she was young and just making her way, she'd taken for a lover the chauffeur to a star, and what a waste of time that had been, but he had been a kind boy.

He picked up his briefcase and escorted her from the waiting room. As he held the door open, she had a feeling that there were other eyes on her. She glanced back before the door was quite closed. The boy backpacker was awake, lying with his head on his rucksack, watching her, amusement in his eyes. He winked.

The kind businessman led her in the direction of the taxi rank, but fortunately he was looking at his watch. She began to limp.

'Oh dear, I've a stone in my shoe. You go on, you mustn't miss your train. I can see the taxi rank. I'll be all right from here.'

He nodded goodbye, and strode off in the direction of the platforms.

She stood behind the Tierack, and watched his train pulling out.

She went back to the waiting room. The backpackers had gone. She took the kind businessman's card from her handbag, tore it in two and flushed it down the toilet.

By four o'clock she had collected Ninety eight pounds. She spent some of this on a coffee and a Danish pastry, and dropped five pound coins into the tin of a boy playing a guitar at the entrance to the station, from sympathy for a

10

fellow artiste.   After that she flushed the train ticket down the loo and changed the script. She had been to a wedding and had lost both her purse and her train ticket home.

By seven o'clock she had One hundred and seventy pounds, give or take. She called it a day and went for her bus.

As she said later that night on the telephone to her best friend, she could not understand those actresses who said there were no good parts for older women. It was just a question of using one's initiative. And having the right hat.

I'll Settle for Arran

Planning for the holiday started one morning early, when the shadows were still long and there was a suggestion of mist over the garden. Marjorie was settled in her usual chair in the conservatory where she spent most of her time now.

'What I would like is a walking holiday in France,' she said.

Alec sat in the other chair bending over to tie the laces on his outdoor shoes.

'Why France?'

'Sunshine,' she said. 'Lavender fields. Chestnut trees. Elizabeth David food.'

He placed his slippers side by side beneath his chair and straightened up. 'You know I don't like the heat.'

Marjorie didn't answer him. She leaned back in the chair and closed her eyes, the better to picture the Dordogne landscape, no, the Languedoc. She murmured the word, rolling it round on her tongue. Languedoc. She had never been to France.

'Some seasons of the year will be cooler than others.'

'I'm going for the paper and rolls. Do you want anything else?'

He asked this every morning.

Velvet nights. Velvet nights and the chirrup of cicadas.

*

'Your father doesn't think a walking holiday in France is a good idea,' she told Fiona, who had come to lunch with Derek as they did every Sunday.

'It's what I would like to do. Do you remember the walking holidays we had when you were young? He carried

12

you in a sling in front of him. You counterbalanced the rucksack. People used to smile at us on the hills. I would have left you with your grandmother but he wouldn't hear of it. We loved the hills in those days. We never went abroad.'

Derek had picked up a magazine and was turning the pages but Marjorie could see he was not reading, but listening to their conversation. Alec was pretending to be asleep.

Fiona laughed. 'Put me off for life, that did. Thank god you stopped as soon as I became too heavy to carry.'

'You don't remember it,' said Marjorie. 'You were much too young.'

'Doesn't matter if I remember or not. There's the photos to prove it. Mostly on Arran. It was dangerous. Supposing he'd fallen on his face. He could have crushed me to death. Or overbalanced on a ridge. Or anything.'

'He wouldn't have. He would now, of course. Our days for ridge walking are over. But walking in France would be nice.'

'We can't afford it,' said Alec, who obviously was not asleep at all.

'Another thing I would like,' said Marjorie. 'Would be for you two to get married.'

Derek cleared his throat and concentrated on the page in front of him.

They wouldn't dare answer her back, she knew that. Fiona just muttered, Oh Mum, under her breath and went to clear away the dirty dishes.

*

The minister had taken to calling regularly. Marjorie was an infrequent churchgoer, Alec not at all, but she was a keen member of the women's meeting and was enthusiastic for the fund raising side of the church, constantly knitting and crocheting little things for the fetes and sales of work. There had been a falling off in her productivity lately, and it seemed to Marjorie that as she produced fewer of the baby jackets, the more solicitous the minister became.

'Nobody crochets any more,' she told him one day. 'Don't expect me to.'

'I don't expect you to,' he said. 'I'm amazed you kept it going so long. Such beautiful little things.'

'Little,' said Marjorie. 'Little things. Little life.'

'Never say that.'

'I do say it. But I've decided what I want to do. I've changed my mind about France. I'm going to walk the pilgrim way to Compostella.'

'Don't be daft,' said Alec. 'It's a thousand miles.'

'How do you know?'

'I looked it up.'

Marjorie turned to the minister. 'He looked it up so that he could discourage me. That's what he's about these days. Discouragement. Here,' she turned to Alec suddenly. 'Look out my walking boots. They're in the cupboard under the stair. I want to have a look at them. I may need new ones. Go on.'

He rose and went out. She smiled at the minister.

'Mind over matter, eh?'

'That's the spirit,' he said.

Alec came back with a supermarket carrier. He took out the boots. There was a pair of socks in them, stuffed in and forgotten, from the last time the boots had been used. The boots hadn't been cleaned and the soles were clogged with dried mud. They were in excellent condition.

'Hardly worn,' said Marjorie, leaning back in her chair, and indicating that Alec could return them to the cupboard. 'They're good enough. I won't have to buy a new pair. See,' she said as Alec came back into the room. 'You won't have that expense. Those'll still do. They'll outlast me.'

'The pilgrim way's too long,' said Alec. 'You have to be reasonable.'

'Something shorter,' said the minister. 'Nearer. Iona?'

Marjorie leaned back in her chair and closed her eyes.

*

They met hill walking, on Schiehallion when Marjorie had a quarrel with the man she was with, and was going down on her own. She stood aside to make way for a man coming up and he stopped, for he saw the tears streaming down her face. Are you all right, he asked and she struggled to smile. She had been told she had a lovely smile, and it charmed him, and they continued to talk, and he turned, although he was only one third of the way up, and escorted her back to the car. He told her later it wasn't just her tears. It was the glow in her cheeks and the way the white mist was clinging like a halo round her hair.

She left a note on the windscreen of her now ex boyfriend's car and went off in Alec's. They went into Dunkeld and sat by the river outside the cathedral and talked and talked. She couldn't remember when they stopped talking, but when she said this to him now, he told her not to be daft.

*

She spent hours at the computer, and found the sites which related to pilgrimages to Compostella. She printed off the maps that showed all the routes from all over Europe. True, there wasn't a route from Motherwell but you could start from anywhere. The printouts ran to over a ream of paper.

She made a list of books she wanted and made Alec get them from the library.

'You won't have time to read them,' he told her.

'I'll make the time.'

'I have a theory,' she told the minister when he called. 'That pilgrimages in the middle ages were no more than an excuse.'

He wasn't going to argue with her and smiled encouragingly so that she continued.

'The Church told them that it was a good thing to do a pilgrimage, and life wasn't too great at home, particularly if they were fed up with their wives and children, and a boss telling them what to do all day, and no surplus income. It was easier just to pack some apples and cheese into your pocket and say you were going on pilgrimage. Who would criticise? So off they went and maybe some did go to where they said they would and maybe some didn't. And maybe some came home, and maybe some didn't. And if they didn't come home who was to say they hadn't died on the way, or on the way back. Easier in those days to escape from a life you didn't want.'

'The crusades as well,' said the minister.

'Exactly,' said Marjorie.

*

'Santiago is named after a saint,' said Alec, who had been looking through one of the books on his way home from the library.

'That's right. Iago is Spanish for James.'

'But we're Protestant. We don't believe in saints.'

'You never go to Church. How can you say what you are?'

'But I'm still a Protestant. What do you want to interest yourself in saints for?'

'I'm not interesting myself in saints. I'm interested in. I told you. I want pilgrim ways.'

'It's too long.'

'It's only a thousand miles. And if you . day you do it in a hundred days. People plan it . as to arrive in Santiago just before the feast day. 1 . have to go a bit slower of course. I could maybe walk fiv miles a day, so I would take two hundred days to do it, add a quarter as much again for rest days say two hundred and fifty days, say eight months. Of course I wouldn't particularly bother about being there for the saint's day. That wouldn't matter to me. I don't believe in saints anyway.'

And so she went on planning. She had the weather charts which showed when the weather was best for walking along the various stages of the route, which bits would be too hot in summer and which bits would be too cold in winter. And she made lists of the things which she would take with her, which all had to be packed in one small rucksack, for she wouldn't have the strength to carry a big one, but then being Europe she could wash her tee-shirts and knickers every night and they would be dry in the morning.

The cost wouldn't be a problem, she explained to Alec, for the pilgrim houses along the route were free. She couldn't invariably stay in one, for they might be too far apart for that, but it meant she wouldn't have to pay for accommodation every night.

'Not every night, just some nights,' she told him. 'And of course the food there is simple. Cheese and olives and bread. When you're walking a pilgrim way you don't stuff yourself with fancy expensive food.'

She wanted to practise that now, but since Alec did the shopping he ignored her carefully worked out hand-written

d just bought mince and fish as usual, and a pizza on
ys.

*

Fiona and Derek came in one Sunday looking flushed and
guilty and Marjorie knew they had been up to something.
She found out over their meal.

'Mum,' said Fiona. 'Dad says you're still interested in
this trip to Spain you mentioned.'

Marjorie waited.

'We've booked you and Dad on a holiday there. Week
after next. Fly from Glasgow, nice hotel, full board,
Marbella, you don't have to worry about a thing. It's still
quite cool there at this time of year. It's just for five days.
You should be all right.'

Marjorie spooned some chile con carne onto a plate and
handed it to Derek.

'I don't want to go a holiday to Spain.'

'You said you did.'

'I said I wanted to walk the pilgrim way to Compostella,
where the church of Santiago stands. It's not the same
thing.'

They finished the meal in silence.

*

The minister held her hand. She was having one of her
difficult days and would have liked a bit of silence, but he
seemed to think it was his job to rally her.

'Do you believe in miracles?' he asked.

'No, but you do, presumably. It's your job.'

'There's miracles and miracles.'

'To get to be a saint, you have to have worked miracles.
At least nowadays. Probably the same in the middle ages.'

'Bigger and better miracles in those days. In those days you could.'

'People were more gullible then.'

'Or they saw more clearly,' said the minister. 'But you don't believe in miracles.'

'I know. You just wondered.'

'Alec tells me you're making preparations to go to Spain.'

'He is. They are. I wasn't consulted.'

'They thought that was what you wanted.'

'They got it wrong. As usual. All my life people have been getting it wrong.'

*

Alec told the children she wasn't strong enough to go to Spain, so Fiona and Derek took time off their work and used the holiday instead so as not to lose their deposit. Before they went Fiona kissed her mother and said 'Look after yourself. We'll take lots of pictures and tell you all about it when we get back.'

*

Marjorie lay in bed. Alec sat in a chair beside her, occasionally turning the pages of a newspaper.

But she wasn't asleep. Gently she reached out a hand and touched his. He glanced up and squeezed her fingers and then returned to his newspaper. She sighed.

'Did you clean my boots?' she asked presently.

'Yes.'

'I'll need them.'

'You're not going anywhere.'

'I am, I am.'

A nun looked in at the door, which was slightly ajar, and went away again.

'I'm not, am I? Going anywhere.'

19

'No.'

'Oh well.' She turned her head to look out of the window. 'I could settle for Arran. But when you stop dreaming you're dead.'

*

Alec took her ashes to be scattered on Goatfell. It was a long way up, and he was overweight, and he was peching by the time he reached the top, with the help of his daughter and son-in-law.

Fergus in Love

Kitty's mother was buried on a spring day when the field beside the graveyard was awash with mayflowers and the wind tossed the shadows of clouds and sunshine across minister and mourners.

Fergus stored these details in his head. Later, he would write a poem.

Now! Now! Now I will rescue you from your loneliness, my beloved Kitty. Now you will take wing and fly with me.

He watched her glance round the small gathering, as if counting. There were some girls from her office. The Great Man wasn't there, but then it was only the funeral of his personal secretary's mother.

There weren't many other mourners, only a few from the church or friends of Kitty. Her mother had been of an age where her contemporaries had gone before her. Gone into that bourne, said Fergus to the woman standing beside him. He vaguely recognised her as someone who went to the art class with Kitty. She gave him a lift to the hotel where the purvey had been laid on.

Later, back at the house and alone together at last, he made Kitty a cup of tea. He caught her glance towards the big flat screen in the corner. There was a wildlife programme on tonight which she ordinarily watched. But convention held.

He asked her, what are you going to do now? For irretrievable time is flying, dear Kitty.

What is there to do? She was too near retirement. There's nowhere to go. The next step up from secretary to a great man is not to become a great man yourself.

So, back to work tomorrow. A good job, in with the bricks, secure for life. Once she was ambitious, once she could have stormed the heights. She could do anything now, with no one to be responsible for.

I lay my life at your feet, beloved Kitty. Use me how you will.

Could he take the mattress from her mother's bed to the rubbish tip, in his van? Kitty wouldn't want it used again. Mrs. Jones would help her sort through her mother's clothes and take them to the charity shop.

*

When June came he suggested she remodel the garden. It had been laid out by her father many years before when they first moved into the house. It was designed to be trouble free, low maintenance. It was landscaped with gravel and leylandii, and only the grass needed attention.

They stood in the middle of it and looked round. He produced the sketch he'd made of arbours and ponds and arches, of curving paths and secret corners. He would do the heavy work and she would choose the flowers. Roses and clematis would flow in rampant glory over pergolas and statuary.

He waited, looking down at the top of her head, greying now, as she stood uncertainly in the middle of his dream, trying to visualise it.

No, she said eventually, I couldn't change anything. My father . . . A silent man, her father. Fergus remembered him. A man who liked his newspaper and his pipe, and an occasional bet on the horses, a mild vice he imagined was hidden from both his wife and his daughter, and which they knew about but tacitly ignored.

Is gone, he could have said. And your mother too.

Kitty's mother had not liked Fergus. He believed she'd crushed the life out of her daughter. Kitty had ambitions to be an artist when she was young. The dreams came to nothing, for people like us don't do that sort of thing.

22

He had patience. Soon, soon, the pent up frustration of all these years would burst the dam and he would be privy to the innermost secrets of her mind and heart and soul.

He could wait.

And he could cut the grass. It needed doing every fortnight now, with this wet weather. And after he'd done that he could stay for supper. But no, she wouldn't think about remodelling the garden just yet.

She smiled when he talked of future changes. Who would want her, plain as she was?

I would, my Kitty. Just as you are, mine own to be.

*

For her birthday he gave her an exercise bike. He helped her to shift furniture to make way for it, to give it pride of place in the middle of the living room.

She could watch television while she exercised. Or exercise while she watched television. This would help her to lose weight.

They could move together into a little cottage where they would live like squirrels in their nests, united against the world.

She was not against the world. Was she? What had she to be against the world about? She quite liked her work. The political party she and her mother had voted for all their lives was in power.

There were the snails of course. They were a nuisance.
Snails?

They come in the bathroom window. She didn't like keeping it closed but if she left it open she quite often found at least one snail crawling along the window sill.

She couldn't stand the things. Was there anything he could do?

Perhaps if she spread barbed wire on the window sill outside that would deter them. They didn't like rough surfaces.

Or sandpaper, perhaps.

Or shards of glass.

Or salt. Salt kills them.

*

They sat in the evening on the patio watching the sun set behind the leylandii.

You'll remember this moment, my Kitty. Store it up, the shadows, the scents, the colours. Bring the memory out in tranquillity and treasure it when we are in the twilight of our lives.

The bin men come tomorrow, she said. Can you put the wheelie out for me before you go?

*

In the queue in the chemists, while he was waiting to pick up her blood pressure pills, and his heart medicine – heart! If they could only see his heart and how it beat red blooded with the thought of his beloved – Mrs Jones remarked how happy Kitty looked, how carefree. Her mother's death was a blessing really.

And him. He was looking peaky. Was he well? We're all getting on a bit.

Were people talking about them? Why was he round at her house every waking hour, doing things for her, worshipping at her feet, now that her mother was no longer there to chaperone them?

How glorious, he thought. To be infamous, to be daring. Two souls meeting as one to defy convention.

Sometimes, sleepless, he walked in the quiet night past her house. Her radio would be faintly playing, but her light

24

would be out. She would have fallen asleep leaving it on. It would rouse her, perhaps, at three in the morning when sleep is lightest, and she would turn it off and lie awake. And would she think of him?

Death comes in the small hours, when human resolution is at its weakest. The idea tore at his heart. His poems became elegies.

*

Come with me, Kitty, let us walk hand in hand on a wild beach beside a wild sea and dance through breakers that stir the stones which are older than man, older than the world. We shall talk of the future and plan our lives.

But Kitty had already arranged to go on a coach trip with a couple of girlfriends.

She owed it to them. It had been promised for some time. It was a treat for Mrs. Jones. A reward for sitting with Mother to let Kitty go to the art class.

Then I will go by myself to a sunsurfed island and think of you. Will you think of me?

Of course.

And would she take her sketchbook and watercolours? She would, and then he could see what she had painted. It would be as good as seeing the places himself. He could use his imagination.

*

In the autumn it seemed to Fergus that Kitty was becoming dreamy. This was unlike her and he said so.

On 14th November it would be twenty five years since she first started working for the Great Man.

And?

And she considered what a privilege it had been, what a joy.

He is but your employer, Kitty.

She would paint his picture and present it to him.

Would he sit for her?

No, no, she could do it from photographs.

Did she have photographs of him?

She went into her bedroom and came back carrying several large scrap books. He recalled the cherubs and angels which little girls traded with one another in the long ago, when they were both young.

She turned the pages. There were photographs of the Great Man in every possible stance. He stood awkwardly in a group, a young man at the edge. In later photographs he moved nearer and nearer the middle of the photo and in so doing acquired girth and gravitas.

There were photographs opening hospitals and closing fetes. Royalty chatted to him. Prime Ministers shook his hand.

These were the official scrapbooks then? No, only Kitty's. She would paint the Great Man's picture, she said, and give it to him, in remembrance of their twenty five years together.

In what sense, together?

She blushed. She meant she worked for him for that length of time. She had shared in his greatness.

And looking at the back of her head, grey and flattened where she had been leaning back against the cushions of her chair, he understood.

Poor Kitty, to carry such unrequited love for so many years. For unrequited he had no doubt it was.

When darkness came he left her and walked towards his house. How could he compete with a captain of industry? No doubt the man knew of Kitty's devotion but chose to ignore it for she was more useful to him as a secretary than as anything else.

Fergus wandered the streets and came to the edge of the town. He took a path through the plantings. Deep in the woods there was a large pond, once used for curling.

Now in the dark and the cold there was no one there.

Farewell, my Kitty. You have broken my heart.

He stepped cautiously forward and his foot sank into mud up over his ankle. He felt the cold water seep through his shoe and sock. He put the other foot in.

Nearby an owl screeched and he leapt in fright.

The cold was beginning to creep up his calves. He took another step forward. The water was even colder but not any deeper.

He recalled that the reason they used to curl here, and indeed skate, was that the pond was no more than two feet deep in the middle and froze easily in winter. Still, one could drown in two inches of water, if one had the will.

Poor Kitty. Would she grieve for him when she heard he was no more? She would know that it was because of her that he had done this. At least, he supposed she would. He hadn't thought to go home and leave a note.

It occurred to him that people would think he had merely gone for a walk in the woods, perhaps with drink taken. He had indeed been for a couple of pints before calling in on Kitty, though presumably it was out of his blood stream now, mostly. But they would think that he was drunk. Even if the post mortem showed that he was not, how many people would read the post mortem report?

And could he inflict such agony upon her?

He stepped backwards. One two three, and he was on dry land again.

He squelched along the path towards home. One day Kitty would be grievously disillusioned with her inamorato, and he would be there to console her.

Or perhaps he would outlive his rival.

Yes, indeed.

He raised his voice and sang, phrases from all the love songs he had ever known.

Refugees

The men came in the early morning, while we were at Terce.

They came from Dumfries, riding up the side of the River Nith to where it joined with our own Cluden Water.

Sister Catherine heard them first. I felt her stiffen beside me and lift her head, and pause in her singing. Then I heard them too, a click of metal hoof on the cobblestones of the courtyard, and the murmur of men's voices, and then silence. They were waiting.

I felt maggots crawling in my belly.

Mother Prioress hadn't heard. Neither had Sister Theresa, who was watching the way her breath fluttered the candle in front of her, a vacant expression on her face. I could tell by the movement of her lips that she was singing the wrong words, or no words at all.

Gloria in exelsis deo et in terra pax hominus bonae.

Our singing was thin, lost in the dark cold of the chapel. Mother sang the amen slowly. There was silence save for the guttering noise of the tallow candles. The whole priory stank of this tallow. It was all we had, after Sister Judith died of the black death, and the bees swarmed and were taken by others.

Mother rose from her knees. Sister Catherine's hand under her elbow was gentle, for touching Mother caused her pain.

Outside, the sun was barely above the horizon. The men had turned their horses onto the stubble of the barley field, and were lounging in the courtyard. They straightened up as we approached. One man turned and spat into the well.

'Lady Blanche,' the Earl's steward greeted Mother.

'You have a message for us.'

'I have to do it,' he said.

She nodded to him and we waited.

He took the parchment from his pouch and read it aloud.

To his Holiness Pope Clement. From his Grace the Earl Archibald Douglas, Lord of Galloway. This the 23rd day of September in the year of our Lord 1389. Concerning the nuns of Lincluden Priory.

A petition that the said Priory be closed and the nuns moved elsewhere. These women have now taken to leading dissolute and scandalous lives, allowing the beautiful monastic buildings to fall into disrepair and ruin through neglect, while they dress their daughters, born in incest, in silk with gold ornaments and pearls.

'That's not true,' I cried.

He paused and caught my eye. I should have lowered my head, as all my life I had been taught to do in the presence of men, but I did not. I stared back at him.

'Go on,' said Mother.

'You could take the rest as read.'

'No,' said Mother. 'Go on.'

He went on with his reading.

The number of nuns including the prioress is reduced to four and they neglect the observances of the day and night offices, devoting their time to the spinning of wool. The local neighbours, who are very evil men, repair to the monastery or to a house about a mile distant from it where they hold a market and even commit incest.

I saw Mother close her eyes for a moment. I saw Catherine looking bewildered. Theresa, as usual, had disappeared.

'It is God's will,' said Mother.

I was speechless with anger.

The steward rolled up his parchment. 'The consent has come from the Holy Father. Your priory is to be closed.'

The men left. One week, said the steward.

Later that day, I walked into Dumfries.

I found Baillie McBraer in conversation with the mason.

The new castle they were building to defend the town against the English already rose four storeys high, the thick walls nearly complete. As I approached, another block of red sandstone was being raised, pulled up by a windlass on top of the wooden scaffolding.

Baillie McBraer saw me, and with a word dismissed the mason.

'Sister.'

'Baillie. I've come about the payment for the barley. We are in need of it now.'

'Oh, aye. A moment, lady.' He turned to give a signal to some men manoeuvring a cart with more stones in it. 'Further over,' he called out. 'Give me two minutes, I'll be with you.'

He turned back to me. 'Do you like our new castle, Sister? A fine building.'

'The English will find it hard to burn,' I said.

Baillie McBraer made a derisive noise in his throat.

'English. They'll not come over the border again. Not now Lord Archibald has shown them they can't do it. A brave soldier, Sister, just like his father before him. But if they do come back,' he waved his hand in the direction of the building work. 'We'll be ready for them.'

It was not many years since I stood with my sisters at the gate of Lincluden Priory and watched Dumfries burning. The people came upriver to us for refuge. We took the women and girls and the babies inside. The men, such few old men and boys as were left from the wars, camped outside in the shelter of our walls.

For several days we waited quietly with the townspeople, watching the clouds glowing red while their timber and thatched houses burned.

Easy burnt, easy built, I remember one woman saying. Happened before, it'll happen again.

Our priory was stone, and we thought it would stand forever.

The Baillie turned back to look at the men working on the castle, signalling to them with snapping fingers.

31

I persisted. 'Baillie, may I have the payment for our grain?'

'Oh that. Might be a bit of a problem paying you.'

'There must be something due to us. There were twenty bushels.'

'But, but, it's like this. I'm told you'll all be leaving the priory, Sister. The Earl's intending to enlarge it, turn it into an abbey, I hear, for monks. They're to say prayers in perpetuity for his ancestors. Yes. Well by rights the money belongs to them. I mean, it's not your money personally, is it? You've taken vows of poverty. You'll be going to a new convent, and they'll have received the money for their grain. I couldn't pay it to you, that would be like you getting the money twice. D'you see that?'

I thought of the hours spent turning over the soil, and sowing the barley, and the back breaking labour we'd had of bringing it in.

Perhaps I should have pleaded. Perhaps he wanted me to plead. But I was too proud.

'I'll let Earl Archibald know I'm holding the money. It's here for his new abbot.'

He signalled to the men who were waiting.

'Good day to you, Sister.'

'God with you,' I replied, automatically.

As I walked back through the town, I heard people laughing. Men shouted lewd words at me. Once they would not have dared. I walked out of the town, my cheeks burning, trembling with anger.

I knew that when the priest came I should confess this, for anger is a sin, but the priest never came. He used to come once a week to the priory to say Mass and hear our confession, but after this we never saw him again.

During the week that was left to us Sister Catherine, Sister Theresa and I sorted through the few clothes we had, and chose the warmest, and heavy woollen cloaks, and the best and soundest of our boots. We packed some food for the journey ahead of us.

Mother knelt at her stall in the chapel, praying, as long as she was able.

Catherine followed me around all the time. Every time I lifted my head from my task, there she would be, whitefaced and frightened.

'I have never lived anywhere but here.'

She had come to the monastery as a baby. Her mother had been one of the many, oh so many women who had died of the plague. Catherine had survived and had been brought here, for there was no one to care for her.

I took her hand and held it.

'There will be somewhere for us. There will be another monastery, with sisters of your own age, and we will be made welcome.'

We were ready when the soldiers came a week later. They dragged our bedstraw out and the straw from the refectory, and burned it, laughing as they crushed the cockroaches underfoot. They took our cow and our handful of hens, and the pewter vessels from the chapel and the kitchen. Such silver as we once had was long gone. They loaded everything that was in the priory onto bullock carts, and sent them away.

The four of us stood outside the walls and watched as they destroyed our home.

'What arrangements have been made for us?' I asked the captain of the soldiers.

He did not know of any arrangements.

'But where are we to go?'

'I was told you had friends who would take you in.'

'We have no friends. Not with the lies the Earl has been telling about us.'

He shrugged. It was none of his business.

I was in despair.

Winter was nearly upon us. What were we to do?

It was no use going to Dumfries for help. Whether the people believed the Earl or not didn't matter. They would not take us in, for fear of his anger.

Mother was standing in the roadway, her eyes closed, praying. The two young girls waited by her side.

Mother opened her eyes. 'We will go to Whithorn,' she said. 'To where the bones of the blessed St. Ninian lie in the cathedral. That will be our new home.'

I argued. Whithorn was too far. It was a long way away, and winter was nearly on us. But Mother had faith. She had faith enough for all of us. When she was only a girl, she had left her family in the north to devote her life to the worship of God, and she knew He would not desert her now. How could I tell her that, God's help or not, she did not have the strength to walk anywhere? She did not see herself as stooped with age and crippled with rheumatism.

Besides, I had been taught to obey Mother Prioress in all things.

I wrapped her cloak more tightly round her.

Then Mother, who had not left the priory for over forty years, turned her face to the west, and picked her way carefully over the rutted track, without once looking back.

Catherine was crying, quietly, the tears pouring down her face.

Theresa said. 'I'm not going.'

'You must,' I said. 'There is nowhere else.'

'There is,' she said.

A lad was waiting in the road, dressed in poor rags, carrying a shepherd's crook. Theresa bent down and undid the pack at her feet, and pulled out Mother's clothes which I had given her to carry.

'Theresa, you don't know what you're doing.'

She smirked at me. She patted her belly.

'Oh yes I do,' she said. 'Better than you.'

34

I looked after the two of them, the boy and Sister Theresa, walking down the track together towards Dumfries, and realised how blind I had been.

Catherine was packing Mother's clothes into her own pack. She slung it on her back and followed after Mother.

'Where is Theresa going?' Mother asked.

Catherine answered before I could. 'She has friends in the town. They will look after her.'

'People are good,' said Mother. 'May the saints bless them.'

I cut staffs for Mother and with one in each hand she was able to walk, but it was her needs which determined our pace.

At first our travel was not too difficult, for people still took their carts and beasts into Dumfries for the market there, and this had kept a road open, rutted and uneven though it was. But as we travelled away from Dumfries, into rougher country, west towards the mountains, it became more difficult.

In places there were tracks, remnants of the old pilgrim road, but this was long disused, for there had been too many years of war. No one travelled now.

In the forests we were sheltered from the worst of the wind and rain, but the way was difficult and the going slow as we followed paths made by deer and rabbits to avoid undergrowth and bramble.

On the open moorland we stumbled our way through heather and bracken and learned that smooth ground was often treacherous with unexpected black bogs into which we were sucked up to our knees.

We often had to climb higher to find a place where we could ford a fast flowing burn, and then slowly make our way again down the hillside, legs and shoulders aching.

We saw few people. Their houses were hidden in folds in the hills, and with winter coming they had taken their animals inside. Sometimes we saw wild goats, and deer, and heard the scream of a pheasant, but the land was almost deserted.

Sometimes we came across an empty ruinous house and we had shelter for the night and remnants of timber to build a fire. But often we had to sleep in the open, in the protection of trees, or under overhangs of rock.

Catherine fared best, being young and strong, and for many miles she would carry all the packs, while I supported Mother.

She and Mother never wavered in their confidence that we would reach Whithorn.

'Once,' Mother told Catherine. 'All the roads round about were black with pilgrims going to the shrine of St. Ninian. Thousands of pilgrims. They came by sea from Ireland and France and Spain. Some came from Flanders through England and walked this way, singing praises as they travelled.'

'What's Whithorn like?' asked Catherine.

'A great city. A great cathedral.'

'And food?'

'A lot of food.'

Catherine was always hungry. She would run ahead and dive into the woods through which we passed, searching for berries. She found brambles and blaeberies and gathered them in her kerchief, to share with us. She found mushrooms, which I added to the mess I cooked every night.

I kept us moving for already the air was cold, and the burns we had to cross sometimes had thin sheets of ice at the edges. I bullied and cajoled, and almost wept when Mother insisted we sing the Divine Office whenever she judged the hour was right. Inside I fumed at the waste of energy and the delays when we stopped, but what could I do?

At the end of each day every muscle and bone ached till we could barely stand.

But as the days passed in a blur of exhaustion for us, and pain for her, soon our praise was only a prayer when we woke in the morning, and Vespers before we settled to try and sleep. We did not sleep well. The ground was hard and when the fire died down it was cold. Sometimes in the night we heard wolves howling.

Our food was finished on the ninth day.

There came days when we walked with no food in our bellies. Sometimes Catherine found berries, but they were blackening with the cold, and scarce. Once a buzzard dropped from the sky in front of us and we saw its talons close over a rabbit. We shouted and it dropped the rabbit and flew away, and the poor animal, injured and easily killed, gave us a good meal that night.

We had to keep walking, walking.

Each day we covered less and less ground. Mother's joints became swollen and hot to the touch. Each night I carefully took off her boots and massaged her feet.

Our boots, which had been made from the skin of our pig the year before and had seemed so strong at the priory, cracked and tore with the rain and the rough stones. Early on, I ripped up our wimples, and Mother's beautiful white cap, the badge of her office, to make rags to bind round our feet.

After that we wore our shawls over our shaven heads. Catherine's hair grew, and mine, but Mother's did not.

Mother and Catherine talked, while I lay silent and anxious.

'The good Lord and his mother will take care of us,' I could hear Mother whispering. 'And the good St. Ninian, he wants us there, where his bones are.'

'Are we on the right road, Mother?' asked Catherine.

Mother had no doubts. We were to keep travelling west and we would arrive at the sanctuary of Whithorn.

We had been avoiding people, for shame that they knew our story, and fear that they would harm us. We had been told stories of outlaws in the hills, men who had deserted the fighting, and who would kill any travellers.

But we needed food, so we sought out people and we became beggars.

We came to a hamlet, no more than three or four houses beside a lochan, and I made the others wait in the shelter of some beech trees, out of sight.

I knocked at the first door and when it was opened a crack I asked for food.

'Be gone with you,' the man shouted and banged the door closed.

I waited till I stopped shaking and approached another door. Two dogs ran out and one sank his teeth into my thigh. I screamed.

There was shouting from inside the house and a woman appeared. She called the dogs off.

'Goodwife, we are three women travelling the road to Whithorn. We have no food. Can we beg a crust?'

She shouted something incomprehensible at me, but it was not friendly.

I stood my ground and she shouted again, this time in a language I could understand.

'We have no food ourselves.'

That night when Mother and Catherine were asleep I was able to rub salve into my leg. My clothes were thick, for we wove strong cloth in the priory, but my leg was badly bruised. And then I could allow myself some tears.

But many times people were kind, and gave us bread, and sometimes oatmeal, and the porridge I made filled our bellies and helped us to sleep.

The weather grew colder and the rain driving in from the north made everything wet and chill. There was nothing dry that would take a spark from my flint, and often we did not have a fire. Mother suffered grievously.

At night I lay with her in my arms to keep her warm, and to cushion her old fleshless bones. I could hear the wheezing in her chest. It had been there for some days. The medicines I had carried for her were done, and there were no herbs to make up fresh.

My heart was full for I loved her as if she had been my real mother. She was my Mother in Christ, and I knew she was going to die.

One day when I smelt peat burning I left the others and followed the smell till I came to a house of mud and stones and turves for a roof. There was no sign of anyone. From the byre there was a clatter and the constant bleat of a goat in heat.

Poor as they were, they had warmth and shelter and we had none.

I lifted the latch and opened the door cautiously. When there was no sound, no shout of protest, I entered. There was no one there. In one corner the peat fire smouldered, and my eyes smarted with the smoke which drifted across the room in the draught from the open door. When my eyes grew accustomed to the dimness I could make out the pallet bed in one corner, and the chair near the fire, and the spinning wheel and a fleece with the carder lying on top of it.

On a bench near the fire also there was some food. I stepped nearer. There was a piece of cheese wrapped in a cloth. Nearby was a tub and when I moved the straw which lay on the top I found that it contained apples.

The smell of the apples brought back the scent of the orchard at Lincluden and I lifted one and bit down hard on it, the juice running down my chin, and the pieces nearly choking me.

I grabbed the cheese, and filled my pockets with apples. There was also a bowl full of oatmeal, and I emptied this into my kerchief and knotted it. I ran out to where Mother and Catherine waited and hurried them away.

We had walked a short distance when we met a woman coming in the opposite direction. She was old and stooped and walked slowly, with a stick, and she was leading a stinking billy goat. She paused and would have spoken, I think, but I hurried the others on, save for a brief greeting.

I felt my sin grievously then, for she had the look of a woman who would have given us the food, and I prayed that when she found her house violated she would forgive these starving strangers.

Afterwards we all had stomach pains from the apples, but Catherine said it was better than the stomach pains from hunger.

The next morning Catherine woke soon after me. Mother was still asleep.

'The people there were kind,' said Catherine.

'Where?'

'Back there. To give you so much food. Couldn't we go back and see if we can stay there for a while. We could work to earn our keep.'

'No.'

'Why not?'

'I stole the food.'

There was silence, save for Mother's snoring.

'You stole it?'

'Yes, I stole it.'

I caught the expression of disgust on her face.

'D'you think I'm proud of it? God knows, the woman had little enough.'

'That was terrible.'

'Would you rather starve to death?'

'What will Mother say when she finds out?'

'She won't find out. You won't tell her.'

'She'll say it's a sin.'

'You will not tell her.' I spoke the words slowly and gripped Catherine's arm as I spoke. She shook me off.

'Deo gratias, my daughters,' Mother greeted us as usual when she woke.

'Deo gratias, Mother.'

All that day I did not leave the two of them alone together.

The next morning, when I awoke, Catherine had gone.

I told Mother that she hoped to find a better road to Whithorn, and would come back to us if it was easier.

It was hard without Catherine.

The days had grown very short, for we were now nearly at the winter equinox, and the long, long nights were dark and cold. Sometimes, when Mother was asleep in my arms and I could not move for fear of disturbing her, I lay with my limbs numb and looked up at the stars, and thought about Mother's enduring faith. She had no doubt that God and his son and St. Ninian were guiding us and protecting us on our journey, and with all of them to care for us, how could we come to harm?

Sometimes in the cold light of the moon, I saw shadows move and heard sounds, and told myself they were only the night time animals, but sometimes in my half-dozing state I could imagine them to be the goblins of legend come to get me. I remembered the stories of ghosts we used to tell in the priory when I was a girl. This annoyed the older nuns, who called us silly and superstitious. But I think they did it too when they were young. And surrounded by the safe stone walls of our priory, we could find the stories thrilling but meaningless. Now, they came back to me in all their horror.

I was always thankful when the first streaks of red began to lighten the sky in the east.

Then suddenly Catherine was there again.

I put my arms round her and she rested her head on my shoulder and we did not say anything for many minutes.

'Here,' she said, unwrapping her pack. She handed me some bread, and some dried fish.

'And here,' she said, and pulled out a phial. I opened it. Wintergreen. Other things. 'Will this help Mother? Is it the right stuff?'

'It will ease her breathing.'

41

Mother was still asleep. I held the phial under her nose and I rubbed some of it on her breast.

When she woke her breathing became easier and her eyes were brighter.

She cried to see Catherine back and clung to her,

We went on. Later, as we rested and ate and Mother dozed again, I asked Catherine, 'Where did you get the food and the medicine?'

'Does it matter?'

I was instantly alert.

'Don't tell me you stole them.'

'No, I paid for them.'

'What with. You don't have anything.'

She was silent. I reached out and took her hand. 'What did you pay with.'

She pulled away. 'It was the only thing I had.

'I walked south for a long time after I left you. I was angry. What you did was a sin, and I thought I would rather die than commit such a sin. But I did not know that begging was so difficult. I tried it, but I was too frightened, and people looked too rough.

'I came to a house that stood by itself. There was a man milking a goat. He gave me a bowl of milk. Do you remember the taste of warm milk, fresh from the cow. I thought I had never tasted anything so good and never would again.

'I could have gone on then, but I didn't. I could smell meat cooking inside the house, and it smelled so good, and I had been hungry for so long. He took me inside and gave me some of the meat. He had medicines too. I saw these things and knew they would help Mother.

'And I thought, I can no longer bear being hungry and cold, and I do not want to beg and I cannot steal, so I will have to pay for them.

'He kissed me on the lips and I didn't know what to do after that, but he made me lie down on the bed and he did things to me, like an animal.

'He said afterwards he was sorry for I couldn't stop crying, and he helped me to clean myself up. But it wasn't his fault. I offered myself.'

Her mouth twisted with the pain of telling it.

'His wife is dead. His two sons were taken for soldiers to fight the English and they've never come back. He has fought too, in the service of Lord Archibald, and was injured. He wanted me to stay.

'But then I ran away and found you again.'

From time to time that night I heard her give a gulping sob, but she slept.

The next day Mother's breathing was easier. I carried her now. She was so light that I could lift her in my arms, and with Catherine leading the way to choose the easiest paths we made progress.

We no longer sang the praises of God.

And then we came to a glen, sheltered from the north wind.

In front of us in the gloaming we could see the bulk of a large building, with surrounding walls, and here and there the flicker of torches.

'Is this Whithorn?' asked Catherine.

We made our way to a torch burning in a sconce in the wall. This marked the location of the door, and beside it a bell gleamed in the light of the flame. I seized the clapper and rang the bell, and we waited.

The door opened and a man in the dress of a lay monk stood there.

'What is this place?' I asked.

'Dundrennan Abbey.'

Dundrennan, where the White Monks lived. We were a long way off our road. We must have come too far south, but I did not care.

I told him who we were.

'Wait,' he said.

I had heard of this Abbey, spoken of with awe for the strictness of the Order. Their founder observed the most severe austerity, forgetting perhaps that our Lord Jesus had not lived in poverty, only in simplicity, and that what is right for the warm south is not necessarily suitable for a cold northern country.

We waited, shivering. All the light had now gone from the sky, and distantly we could hear Vespers being sung in deep men's voices, strange to our ears. Beside me Mother was murmuring the words to herself. Catherine and I were silent.

The door opened and we were invited in.

In the porch the almoner waited. He bid us welcome, but his voice was flat and dry, and I knew he had heard the story of our priory and that we were not welcome here.

'We have some accommodation for travellers,' he said.

'Thank you.'

'No doubt you will be moving on tomorrow.' He led the way, lamp flickering, along a dark passageway and showed us to a room where a number of pallets were laid out.

'Please,' I said. 'We need a fire for Mother. She is ill.'

'Ill?' This was said sharply.

'Ill with a congestion in the chest. Nothing catching.'

'I will send someone, and food and water. Goodnight Sisters.'

A lay brother brought a brazier, and built up a fire in the hearth. I thanked him and he looked at me sideways and scuttled away, without speaking.

Soon, with the door closed, the room began to warm up. The food the brother brought was simple, bread and pease brose, no doubt the same as the brothers themselves were having, and we were grateful for it.

44

We lay on the pallets, and stretched out our limbs in the warmth, and smelled the pinewood and peat of the fire, and fell asleep.

In daylight I could see the abbey was a fine one, larger than our priory, and built of a whiter stone. It lay protected in the hollow made by three hills, and a river ran along the southern edge. In summer, when the trees are clothed in green, it must be a beautiful place.

Our benefactors know that the worship of God is easier when the religious are surrounded by beauty. They choose the best places. No doubt that was why Lord Archibald wanted our priory round which to build his fine new abbey.

For the first time since I left it, I allowed my mind to return in memory to Lincluden, tranquil in the curving arm of the Cluden Water, with the heron standing silently for hours, and the apple blossom in the orchard, and the meadow where our cow grazed. I would never see it again.

Mother became too ill to move and we had to stay.

The Abbot sent a priest, who gave her Viaticum, to prepare her for her final journey.

I watched him as he anointed her brow, her nose, her mouth, her ears and her breast with the holy oil.

The priest and I sat by her bedside through the long watch of the night. Catherine lay on her pallet, her back to us.

Once Mother woke, and I saw her fingers open and curl up. I reached out my hand and put it into hers. She sighed.

'I was walking beside St Ninian. He told me he has been caring for us on our journey. Was I asleep? Was it just a dream, d'you think?'

I stroked her hand, and thought how much I loved her, and thought how unjust it was that she, who had lived a harmless life, worshipping God, should become a wanderer and die in a place where she was not wanted. I thought of how I had become a thief, and of what had happened to Catherine.

45

She drifted into unconsciousness, and towards dawn, she died.

We buried her at noon, in a corner of the Abbey's graveyard, well away from the graves of the monks. The priest intoned the burial service. Only Catherine and I and the almoner were there, and the four lay brothers who lowered her body into the earth.

In all the time we were there I never saw the abbot.

'What will you do?' asked the priest.

'Travel to Whithorn, as we were doing,' I said. 'I hope we will find sanctuary there, and peace.'

'Whithorn is a poor place, now that the pilgrims no longer come. The cathedral is falling into ruin. But I think there are some monks still there.'

'One place is as good as any other,' I replied.

Catherine and I packed up our clothes, such as they were. We were given food for the journey.

The priest was to walk with us part of the way, to show us the road. Half a morning's journey, and we breasted a hill, from where the priest pointed to the line on the horizon which was the sea.

'There,' he said. 'Keep going west. There are two large rivers, but there are settlements at the fords and the people will see you safe across. God be with you.'

He turned and strode back to the abbey.

'Well Catherine,' I said, for this was the first chance we had to talk together alone. 'We are nearly at journey's end, if the priest is to be believed.'

'I'm not going.'

I looked at her.

'I'm going back. I belong to that man now. I'm going back there.'

I seized her hands, as if to keep her with me by force. 'Please Catherine, stay with me.'

'I can't. There is no future for me in Whithorn, or anywhere else with good people. I will go back and serve him and have his children.'

We embraced and then she turned back towards the east.

When she was out of sight, I turned west, towards Whithorn.

I never saw her again.

Waiting for a Death

It was a matter of waiting for a suitable death.

Now I had one. I telephoned Sheena and read out the details.

'How long will it take?' she asked.

'Give it six weeks say, or two months. Depends how busy they are at the passport office. Don't fret. You've waited a while already. Be patient.'

'Are you sure it will work?'

'Positive.'

'I'm not sure.'

I snapped. 'It's me that's putting my career on the line if it doesn't work.'

I examined again the birth and death certificates in front of me. The funeral was over. The family had come to my office for The Reading of the Will. That's what people persist in calling it, though nowadays I never do anything quite as formal. I give my clients a copy of their Will to keep with the bankbooks so the family have it well scrutinised before ever the deceased is underground, or scattered to the wind as this one was.

I now had the bank books, and the insurance policies, and a few more bits of paper, and most importantly, the birth certificate of my client, aged 42, unmarried and never, I knew, been abroad and therefore never had a passport. I love this country, she'd told me during one of the conversations we had when I drew up her Will. I can't see why anyone would want to go abroad. Poor Jean, you've lived your narrow and sadly short life and now I can use your birth certificate and it will take someone further than you've ever been.

It would be too easy.

Sheena and I had been friends since our giggling schooldays, loving and hating over the boys we both fancied. It was the kind of friendship that survives distances, marriages, divorces and temporary misunderstandings. We'd picked up again after she and her husband Campbell bought a house locally and I'd done the conveyancing for them. She'd married him during one of the times we'd been out of touch. The wedding had been all white and silver marquee and stretch limos. I'd seen the wedding photos and it struck me as over the top, even for Sheena, but then Campbell had plenty of money.

Three years isn't long in a marriage, but it's a lifetime in the wrong marriage.

'The novelty's worn off,' she said one day.

'What, of being married?'

'Yes, and all this.' She took a gulp of her wine, somewhat to my distress. It was a smooth Cote du Rhone that she'd brought up from the wine cellar - yes, the house had a cellar and Campbell stored his wine in it.

Lately we'd taken to having lunch together every Friday. After a few sorties to restaurants round about we'd settled into a routine of meeting at her house, where she'd cook something simple, open a bottle of wine, and talk. The house was beautiful. It was Victorian and had been restored with Campbell's money and the guiding hand of an interior designer who'd worked for the National Trust. It set off to perfection the very best modern furniture that could be bought. Do stone and wood and leather have an affinity?

'Are you thinking of giving it up then?'

'God no. But something different. Somewhere else. It's really being married to Campbell I can't stand any more.'

'Does he know?'

'He doesn't want to know.'

I didn't think Campbell was that insensitive, but I didn't argue with her.

'It's gone, what we had,' she told me. 'He doesn't love me anymore. He works all the time. We never go out. I hardly see him. And his temper. You wouldn't believe his temper.'

'He's always nice to me,' I told her.

'He's different outside. You know what they're like. A saint outside and a devil at home. We don't even have sex any more.'

'Then leave him.'

'He won't let me.'

'He can't stop you.'

'Without him I've no money.'

'Get a divorce. I'll do it for you. I'll make sure you get a good chunk of his assets.'

Sigh. 'But he'll fight. And what happens meantime. I can't live without a decent income. And you know I won't get a job. Employers don't take you seriously when you're our age.'

'So you'll stay with him for his money?'

Over months she talked like this. Never reaching a decision, round and round in circles, never making up her mind, and constantly harping on about money.

'I could take my share of the money and go.'

'Steal from him, you mean?' I was startled. This was extreme.

'Yes. Come on, don't look like that. You lawyers. You have to do everything the right way, don't you. It's what the court would give me. You said it was. Half the assets on divorce.'

'Possibly. But not quite that simple.'

'God's sake,' she said. 'Nothing ever is quite that simple with you, is it?'

'I'm sorry. I can't help it. It's just that lawyers do see every side of the question.'

'Well, see my side of it. I could go abroad. I'd like that. Italy maybe. Sunshine. But he'd find me. And kill me.'

'Nonsense, people don't. It's just a figure of speech.'

50

'You don't know Campbell. I'm frightened of him. He's got connections all over. He'd hunt me down.'

'Really, Sheena. Why must you be so dramatic?'

'I could change my name. Assume a new identity.'

The wine was getting to her. I tried to be matter of fact. 'Hardly possible nowadays. We're catalogued from birth to death.'

'I would need a false passport. You could help me.'

'Lawyers always do their best for their clients, but there are limits.'

But the idea ticked away in the back of my mind and the more I thought about it the more realistic it became. Almost without conscious thought I worked out a way of getting a perfectly legitimate passport but in someone else's name. A real government issue passport. That's the advantage of being a lawyer and knowing how things work. You can see all the possibilities.

I described this to Sheena, jokingly. But it wasn't a joke.

'I hate him. I want away from him. Please, let's do it.'

'All right. As soon as someone suitable dies.'

Now someone had, and I had the first requirement. A birth certificate.

'You'll need a passport photo,' I told Sheena. 'Get your hair cut first. It will make you look different. And be careful not to have any more photos taken of you after that.' She wore her hair long then. It made her look a bit like a witch.

I collected a passport application form from the post office, and while I was there I filled in a form for my late client's mail to be forwarded to me, normal practice in my capacity as Executor.

The next afternoon, over a bottle of the very finest claret, for we felt celebratory, I helped Sheena fill in the application form.

My part in it was to swear that the photo of Sheena was the applicant.

For a moment I hesitated. What I was doing was contrary to all my principles, all my training.

Sheena smiled at me and gripped my arm. What would it be like when she was gone? Behind her the willow tree in the garden stirred in the wind and sunshine and shade danced on the french windows which were slightly open. I could feel the tranquillity of the old house.

I certified the photo. It was in a good cause.

Three weeks later the new passport was delivered to my office.

I took it round to her. She was sparkling. She'd been to the hairdresser again, and had her hair dyed. She looked a lot younger. Forty two even.

'I hope you know what you're doing,' I said.

'You're so good to me. Why are you so good to me?'

I was embarassed. 'We've been friends a long time. I don't like to see anyone unhappy.'

'I'll let you have your share of the money.'

'God, no. I don't want it. I've plenty.' I thought, but didn't say it, that's theft, and that I don't do.

'Here's to you,' I lifted my coffee cup in salute. 'And a successful disappearance.'

'It will be,' she replied. 'It's all planned.'

It was three weeks later I passed their house in the morning to see the police car and an ambulance outside. I wondered if she'd gone already. But surely Campbell wouldn't report her to the police. And why the ambulance? And why a constable at the door?

I stopped.

'Move on please madam,' said the policeman. 'You can't park here.'

I gave him my card. 'The family are my clients. What's wrong?' He went into the house and was back in a minute. 'We'll be in touch.'

I wondered how long Sheena had been gone. And why the ambulance?

Because Campbell was dead. That's why. Murdered while he slept, heavily sedated by the pills, which his G.P. at the trial testified had been prescribed for insomnia, and a lot more alcohol in his system than was wise. It was a combination that rendered him comatose while a pillow was pressed to his face till he stopped breathing.

It was the home help who found him. She'd had a phone call from Sheena on the Saturday to say don't come in on Monday or Tuesday, they were being redecorated. Yes, come in on Wednesday and yes there would be a fair bit of mess to clean up. A fair bit of mess, the home help repeated this with relish in her evidence. Yes, indeed.

So Sheena had from Saturday till Wednesday before they even started looking for her. Time enough to be away to God knows where.

I knew of course that with such careful planning and the genuine passport, they would never find her. Not unless they knew the name she was using. And I had the only photo of her with short hair, a copy of the passport photo which I'd dropped into my handbag that day we filled in the form.

I thought about it for a day and a long anguished night. Then I telephoned the police.

So here we both are in prison. I didn't ask for leniency at my trial. I wanted to be here. We're kept apart. Her crime was, after all, much more serious than mine. Making a false declaration on a government form isn't as serious as murder, but it still had to be prison, for the judge reckoned a lawyer ought to know better.

In the meantime, I'm quite enjoying it. I work in the library, and I spend most of my time here, reading and writing and planning.

I've built up a good circle of contacts. Sheena was right about me. I can always find solutions. Most of the women in here have problems I've never come across in my job. I can help them a lot. So I'm really very well thought of.

Some of them would do anything for me. Just now, all I ask is that they pass the message along.

The thing is, she should never have killed him. She shouldn't have killed my Campbell, my lover, my friend, my future. I can't forgive that. She didn't deserve him and she didn't make him happy. Not the way I would have. If she'd just robbed him and gone away we would have had a life together, him and me, and she'd never have been missed. I lie awake at night aching for the loss of him, and planning.

I don't think being in prison is sufficient punishment for her. There has to be more. I'm considering the possibilities.

Lessington Hall

They say ghosts are trapped in the place where they died. I know this to be true.

My name is John. I'm your guide today. I've worked here at Lessington Hall for almost ten years. I started in the spring of the year I'll tell you about later, when I show you the place where it happened.

This has always been my favourite time of year, when the flowers on the rhododendrons are young and strong and waxy, and the leaves on the beech trees are pale green, and there is a kind of breathlessness in the air, on the cusp of spring and summer.

The Hall, as you will have read on the display in the visitor centre, was built by the first earl, a favourite of Anne Boleyn. He was a clever man by all accounts, who kept his head down, and so escaped the purge that followed that lady's downfall. Later earls lacked the discretion of the first, and they have long since disappeared in an excess of debauchery and death duties.

The Hall was no longer owned by the family when I started work here. It belongs now to a pension fund with their registered office in the Cayman Islands. It doesn't say that on the information board in the visitor centre, but then there is a lot that they keep quiet about.

You've seen inside the house? Very fine, isn't it?

The family who built it and lived here for centuries may have lacked moral fibre, but they made up for that with a fine aesthetic in matters of decoration and furnishings. The portraits are by the finest painters of the day. They may not be of the family, but what of it? They're handsome men and women.

The Hall has proved popular with day visitors like yourself, willing to part with a few pounds to look at how the rich and powerful once lived, and to listen to the history of the place told to them by guides like me.

Most of the history we've been taught to recite to the public is true. Not all of it is true about Lessington Hall, of course, but if something has happened some time, some place, then no doubt similar things have happened here, at the Hall, and the stories can safely be incorporated into our spiel without contradiction. You wouldn't dream of contradicting me now, would you, a nice girl like you.

You see I'm letting you into trade secrets I don't usually tell the public.

The particular day of which I speak was in July, a couple of months after I started work here. I was taking a party of teenagers round. One of the other guides took the boys to look at the shooting range in the basement of the house – the late family had been into guns. Some of the girls wanted to see the woods. It was one of those hot languorous days where you seek cool, and quiet, and running water. We came out through the Italianate gardens, and the pleached alley, and down into the woods. We followed much the same path we're following now.

There are twenty four acres of very fine mixed hardwoods. Over there you'll see a couple of specimens of North American redwoods, two hundred years old, brought by the seventh earl, who was a bit of a wanderer.

The bluebells are almost over but you can imagine what a magnificent sight they are when in full bloom. They give way now to meadowsweet and foxglove.

I remember that day. I often relive it in my mind. It was moving towards evening, with the sun slanting through the trees, and making pools of sunshine on the woodland floor, tempting the girls to separate, and wander off one by one into the woods, after their own devices.

I don't know if it had been planned that way. Sometimes, looking back, I wonder whether it was a plot, whether they had marked me out as someone on whom they

56

could play a joke. Do I look the sort of person who would attract a practical joke?

I was left with a slip of a lass, very pretty and I would say about seventeen years old, possibly a bit younger. I find it impossible to judge the ages of you young women nowadays. I had not noticed her in the party, particularly. She seemed to be on her own, not one of them. She was wearing a long filmy dress the colour of honeysuckle, the pink and the yellow flowing into one another. That was the style of clothes that year, clinging, feminine. You're wearing dresses like that again, I notice. Fashion drifts round in circles.

'Would you like to see the lily pond?' I asked her, when she and I were alone together.

'I've seen it before,' she said. 'A long time ago.'

'Come now, my dear, a lady as young as you doesn't have a long time ago in your history.'

'Oh, I do,' she said.

Soon we left the path and picked our way through the trees towards the pond. The path at that time didn't lead straight to the pond, though as you can see it has been opened up again. At that time no one ever went there.

We're within sight of it now. It is one of my favourite places. It's not just a pond, as you can see, more a small lake. You can see the ruin of the boathouse over there, mouldering. There are the remains of a rowing boat in it, unusable now of course. It's all that's left from the days when the family had the house. The pond was stocked with fish then, trout and bream, and the men would fish or pretend to, and take the girls out onto the water, and who could say what was talked about, or what plans were made, safely away from other people.

It was warm, and the air was heavy with the scent of the wild roses. They're coming out now, can you see? It was quiet that day too, except for the hum of the bees and the flies, and the purring of the wood pigeons.

She slipped her hand into mine. It was a cool hand.

'Cold hand, warm heart,' I said.

'Oh no. A cold heart too.'

I knew she was making fun of me. I was old fashioned then, and I was conscious of the uniform I was wearing. I had my position to think about. If I said or did anything, and caused her to complain, I would lose the job, and it has been the best one I've ever had, despite the horrible uniform.

And apart from that, like a lot of young men, I didn't know how to flirt. Perhaps that is something that comes with experience, and I never had the practice.

'How old are you?' I asked.

'Two hundred and twenty,' she said.

It crossed my mind then that she was quite mad.

'Do you think I'm pretty? So many men have thought me pretty.'

'You're very pretty. You're beautiful. More beautiful than any of the ladies in the portraits in the house.'

'Do you think I look like them?'

'No.'

'Oh, some people say I do. I'm descended, you know, from them.'

'I don't believe you.'

'It's true. I could show you my birth certificate.'

'They didn't have birth certificates two hundred and twenty years ago.'

She laughed, a contralto laugh that sent a warm glow through me.

'Don't you get tired of showing people over the house every day? Don't you ever have a bit of fun?'

She was standing very close to me, and she raised her hands and entwined her fingers in the buttons of my jacket and started to undo them.

'Aren't you warm in this jacket?'

She was wearing her hair pinned up in a loose bun at the back with wisps drifting down over her neck and ears. I put

58

my hands up to stroke it. Oh, she was so insubstantial. I could see her shimmering.

She put her face up to mine. She pouted her lips, inviting a kiss. I could see a fine gold down on her cheeks, and her eyes, deep blue, rimmed with black, with long eyelashes. Laughing at me.

I put my hands round her neck and squeezed and squeezed. Her neck looked fine, thin, white like the stem of a dandelion. But it was very, very solid. There was hardly a sound.

When she lay dead at my feet I picked her up and carried her to the edge of the pond. She had no weight to her. I filled her pockets with stones. Such silly little pockets she had in her flimsy dress, never meant to hold anything heavier than one of those lacy handkerchiefs you girls use. They tore as I pressed the stones in. I slid her gently into the pond, and the soft green lily pads closed over her with hardly a ripple.

I see her here a lot. I come sometimes in the late afternoon when the sunshine slants through the trees, and watch her drifting around in her long dress the colour of honeysuckle.

I hanged myself from that beech tree over there. Do you see the branch at just the right height?

Why do you stare at me in such horror? Do you not envy me?

Think about it. For me it is always Lessington Hall, and there are many young girls like you, and for me it is always summer.

Miss Bell and Miss Heaton

The bus dropped them at the road end just as the rain was easing off. It had rained all night, and really it was foolish to be coming out at all, but this walk had been planned for some time. For Jane Bell, secretly and, she suspected, foolishly, it had become the most important part of the holiday.

Their stout shoes kept their feet dry, but their stockings were soon splashed with mud. Dora worried aloud whether if they washed them in the handbasin in the guesthouse bedroom they would be dry for tomorrow. The room was not very warm.

Jane trod steadily forward.

'Perhaps if we just let them dry without washing them we could brush off the mud. Once it's dried,' said Dora. 'It depends on the kind of mud, doesn't it?'

Dora had plans for next year's holiday. They hadn't gone away this year because of course they didn't want to miss Queen Elizabeth's coronation. Next year, she vowed, they would return to France, to Normandy where they had been so many times before the war. She seemed not to question that it would all be just as it was. Jane tentatively suggested that perhaps the area was in some way degraded by the war but Dora wouldn't hear of it. Nothing would have changed, not basically.

Jane was not going to waste time thinking about next year. She had been thinking, instead, about love. When all falls away, love remains, the poet said.

The burn on their left flowed fast and noisily, swollen with the rain, dragging emerald patches of watercress. Like Ophelia's hair, thought Jane.

There was a narrow path, and they walked in single file, Dora in front as always. A pheasant screeched somewhere beyond the trees.

We do a lot of walking, Jane had told her doctor, and he nodded. Keep it up, he said. The subtext had been, you'll need all your strength.

Dora was carrying the old khaki haversack that once belonged to a cousin. When they went walking Jane never carried it, just as she never walked in front. It had always seemed to her to be a small concession to Dora's need to manage everything. Dora was practical. Dora was positive.

Poor Dora, Jane thought now, I will tell her today. It might be easier when we're walking.

'Beware of the bull,' read Dora aloud from a notice. She stopped and peered into the field. 'I don't believe there is one. That's just there to stop people climbing the fence.'

'There's no reason to go into the field,' said Jane.

'But people will try. Particularly children,' said Dora.

Jane was aware of how she and Dora looked to others, Miss Bell and Miss Heaton, middle aged, each in her own way unattractive, living together, the target of sniggers from the older boys in the school.

Dora taught the first, second and third year pupils mathematics. There were no shades of grey in Dora's world. Dora's lessons never varied from year to year. A good grounding was what she swore by. Let Mr. McKenzie teach the older boys the higher reaches of calculus. Her pupils could, and frequently did, achieve full marks in their exams.

It was a precise life. Dora had a precise mind. Not like Jane who sometimes felt the facts of her own subject, history, shimmering and slipping away under her exposition to bored children.

Jane reviewed in her head the arrangements that would have to be made. She had an appointment next week to see her solicitor about her Will. She had a brother, whom she never saw. She once upon a time entertained dreams that

61

perhaps his children would visit often and treat her as a favourite aunt, but it never happened. It would not happen now. She would leave them all something, as a memento. Everything else went to Dora.

But there was so much had to be lived through before then. The first thing would be the removal of her bosoms. Well, that was all right, great useless floppy things anyway. But it wouldn't stop there, and she knew it.

'Penny for them.' Dora had paused to allow Jane to catch up.

'Really, Jane, you look as if you're miles away.'

'Sorry. Wool gathering.'

They walked on. The path widened and they could walk side by side.

Now? No, not now. Wait till we reach the cave.

There are some experiences you can't summon up to order. Love was one of them.

Finding love wasn't like giving the weekly list to the grocer. There was love and there was romance. Romance she understood. In 1911 the young Prince of Wales visited the village and she daydreamed that he would ask to be introduced to the interesting looking girl, and true love would follow. That was romance. She wondered if Dora had ever daydreamed like that. It seemed silly now. It was silly.

But what about the old khaki haversack, bouncing now on Dora's hip as she jogged clumsily down the slope. Dora's cousin had been killed in the Great War. Why should she have claimed his haversack, and kept it? There were so many things she had never asked her friend, and never would now, for what would be the point of her knowing?

The way was narrowing and the burn and the path began to intermingle. They had to pick their way carefully, stepping on stones to keep their feet dry.

'Don't fall in,' said Dora.

They turned a bend and suddenly through a cleft in the land there was the sea, glimmering blue.

The tide was out, exposing the rocky, pebbly beach, with great swathes of stones rubbed to perfect spheres and eggs by the action of the waves. Dora hardly paused, but walked on, the stones shifting and grinding under her feet.

Jane went further down the beach, picking her way over small areas that were finer, sandier, through the patches of seaweed and detritus washed up by the sea. Here, unsheltered, the wind plucked at her skirt. She stood, breathing deeply, her face raised to the sky, savouring the wind and the faintest suggestion of rain on her face. There was a strong subterranean current and a heavy swell caused the waves to crash onto the land, with scatterings of white spume which refracted the light and floated like little rainbows.

Ahead of them was the saint's cave which had been visible since they stepped onto the beach. It was a large triangular fissure in the cliff.

'Good fertiliser,' called Dora.

'What?'

'Seaweed. Good fertiliser for the garden. Full of nitrogen.'

Jane followed her friend towards the cave.

There were no mysteries here. It wasn't a deep cave, just a triangular gap in the cliff, deep enough for half a dozen people to stand or sit. It wasn't dark or mysterious, but light and dry, and the enclosing rock was the colour of honey.

She passed through a sparkling curtain of raindrops falling from the rocks above. The floor was sandy and clean. The air smelled fresh. There were no corners where horrors could lurk.

It was not what she was expecting.

Most unexpected of all were the memorials. On the ledges created by the long ago movement of the rock, there were simple crosses, some merely twigs bound with twine, some more substantial, showing the labour of creation. In some fissures were posies of flowers and grasses, dried to brittleness. There were stones placed too, small stones from the beach, gathered for their meaningful shape or colour and placed here as hillwalkers place a stone on top of a cairn, but these were individual, isolated, each a memento of a visit to the cave by someone to whom it meant something. Perhaps they were there to give thanks, or seek solace, or the answer to a problem.

But some problems have no answer.

'Do you believe in faith healing?' Jane asked.

'Of course not. Sentimental nonsense.'

She reached out a hand to a stone placed over a piece of paper, but didn't disturb it. She could read *For J asschendaele 1917 aged 19*. Passchendaele. Correctly spelt, the dominie part of Jane's brain noted. In 1917 Jane had been seventeen years old and if she had been a boy she might have been at Passchendaele. If she'd been older, she might have had a lover who died there. But she was a girl and so she stayed at home and survived to grow middle aged teaching boys and girls to pass exams with facts which would be of no use to them in their futures, and many of those children had grown to fight and die in another war. And she had never had a lover, to live or to die.

The paper under the stone was hardly discoloured. It had not been there long. This death was still being mourned. *For J John? Jim? Passchendaele 1917 aged 19.*

'Jane,' called Dora.

Jane turned. 'Smile,' said Dora, bending her head over the Box Brownie.

In her turn, Jane took a snap of Dora standing at the entrance to the cave. Dora dropped the haversack at Jane's feet and went off down the beach to look for stones.

Lovers. When she was young she had been ignorant of physical desire. There had been a boy at university. They'd gone to concerts together and he'd kissed her when they said

64

goodnight, but something must have been wrong with her responses because he married someone else.

Plain Jane. Plain by name, plain by nature, her father used to say. He meant it as a compliment.

Her friendship with Dora was stronger than affection, there was no doubt about it. But was it strong enough to be called love? She supposed it was. And presumably mutual. How else would they have put up with one another all these years? But was it the kind of love that people who called themselves lovers felt?

When she and Dora were younger they had often shared a bed on holiday, for they couldn't afford two rooms. It was common enough in those days when a bed of one's own was a luxury. There had never been any physical contact between them that was not chaste and useful. Nursing each other when they had flu, helping Dora to dress that time she broke her arm. An occasional hug when one or other of them was grieving over the death of a friend or a relative.

Dora sometimes referred to old romances. Sometimes, in company and in conversation when appropriate, she would laughingly remark she had a boyfriend once who . . . And there would follow some amusing, occasionally unkind, anecdote about some nameless young man of long ago. She had certainly been popular at university. And there had been the cousin whose haversack she still cherished.

Would life have been different if she and Dora had been lovers? More fulfilling, perhaps, though in what way she couldn't quite imagine.

If she and Dora had been lovers, would Dora have noticed the lump? Would she have urged Jane to go to the doctor sooner? Would that have been a good thing or a bad thing? So many questions. She would have had support in the ordeal she had already faced alone in the doctor's surgery, taking in only half of what he was saying to her.

On the other hand in a crisis Dora could be a pain in the neck. Cheerful, competent, managing, controlling. Fine when you needed it, but exhausting sometimes. Perhaps there were some things it was easier to face alone.

But now she would have to tell her.

Jane watched her friend bend down, straight back, bottom in the air, to pick up a stone. Dora collected stones. She had an interest in geology. She found something interesting and held it up to indicate this to Jane.

Jane waved back. She began to untie the string that held the flap of the haversack. Their landlady had given them a pack of sandwiches and a thermos of tea.

Now Dora would come up from the beach claiming to be hungry.

They would eat their lunch first, and then Jane would tell her.

Shoes

Chrissie's right shoe developed a hole.

She hated the public ordeal of buying shoes. Who ever had the confidence to ask for a private fitting room? Perhaps only people who shopped at Harrods could, but then perhaps the very rich had shoes that never wore out.

Her sister, who worked in a shoe shop one summer, told her the girls never stooped down to help the customer try on the shoes. The smell, she said.

She blushed for her swollen ankles, her bunion and support stockings. Perhaps if she lost weight her feet would somehow become smaller, or at least neater.

She disliked the self service shops where you browse through single shoes on racks, make a choice, and stand on one foot to try it on, blocking the aisle. She went there once, and the very idea puts her in a panic.

Nor could you buy shoes by mail order, unless you wanted to order twenty pairs and return nineteen, and even then no guarantee of a good fit. No one has yet invented the crimplene equivalent for shoes, stretchable in every direction.

On Sunday she went to church and knelt in prayer. Not for Chrissie the modern half crouch. She was kneeling properly. Thus the soles of her shoes were exposed to the stranger who sat behind her.

As they left the church he pressed some banknotes into her hand with the words 'Buy yourself some new shoes, honey.'

When he was out of sight, she dropped the money in the Cats Protection League collecting box.

In the matter of buying shoes, she reflected, you're embarrassed if you do, and embarrassed if you don't.

Long Road to Iona

When Christopher ran away the first time, when he was eleven, he took cheese and pickle sandwiches he'd made himself and some money from my purse.

I've taken nothing from anyone.

I'm properly clad. My boots are comfortable, my clothes are warm, my rucksack's light.

I have nothing.

I want nothing.

I am nothing.

I walk.

Sometimes I meet other walkers on those bits of the country where everything is purple moorland. Sometimes they're hill walkers coming off the hill, or in the early morning going in. Often, nearer villages, on paths by rivers, I meet people with dogs. They often speak. They don't think it odd to see a woman walking alone. The clothes are a disguise of sorts.

In trousers and fleece you are as anonymous as everyone else. If I was mincing along in high heels and diamante jacket people might think it odd. They might think I'd escaped from the nearest old folks home.

*

The best time on the farm was the early morning. Ian rose early but I rose earlier, and went through to the kitchen from our cold bedroom. The kitchen would still be warm and it didn't take much to tickle the Aga back into life.

The first cup of coffee in the morning was the best. No other all day tasted like it. I ground the beans fresh. That coffee grinder was a wedding present. I wonder what happened to it. Wonder if the daughter-in-law has it.

In winter I would sit in the warmth of the kitchen with my feet up on the towel rail of the Aga, warming my bum. Magic. But the summers were best, when I could take my mug outside and sit on the bench at the front of the house, where I could see the glen running down to the beech trees that marked the course of the river, and feel the warmth of the sun, and listen to the birds. Everything would be quiet, except for the birds. I don't remember any windy mornings. Only stillness, and warmth in the sun. It was my time.

Christopher called it my meditating. For years I went to a yoga class on a Wednesday night, and every morning I would stretch and breathe and then settle down. I didn't call it meditating. That was Christopher.

He was laughing at me, but he understood. He used to disappear down to the river for hours.

The daughter-in-law. She never calls me anything. Not Jean, not mother, not mum. Behind my back she calls me my mother-in-law. I've heard her on the phone to her friends. My mother-in-law. Possessive. I'm not anybody's *my* anything. When the child was born I expected her to start calling me gran, or nannie, but she didn't do that either.

She wanted Tom to go and live with her, but he couldn't do that. He couldn't go because your home is your work when you're a farmer. So to get him she had to marry him and come and live in the farmhouse. Tom was going to inherit the farm. The daughter-in-law had to make some sacrifices.

It was what I did, after all, when I married Ian, and I hadn't liked it then, but I was faced with the same choice, which wasn't a choice.

She's forgotten it was my generation that tested the pill for them. We were the guinea pigs, the ones who got thrombosis and cancer and all the rest of it while the scientists experimented with the oestrogen and the progesterone and every combination of pill. And then we tested the HRT for them. She should be grateful.

Young ones think they know everything.

*

There wasn't any warning. That day he was just working away as usual, and then he had his tea and lit his pipe and then said Jean I've got an awful bad pain in my chest, and he was dead before the ambulance could find us. Not surprising, when you think that our road was called one thing officially but everybody local called it something different, and we were hard to find unless you knew. The road never had any name on it till the council put up the signs at the end, which surprised everybody for we never knew it was called that. But that put the ambulance men off. Maybe it wouldn't have made any difference.

I wanted to keep him in the house till the funeral. They could have brought the coffin and he could have lain in our room. It would have been right. But the daughter-in-law, her that knows everything, said the undertakers had to get him back to their place right away for they have to do their work before rigor mortis sets in, otherwise they have to break his bones to straighten him out.

I scattered his ashes in the front garden, where I could see them when I sat with my coffee in the morning. Beigy powder. It was like he was keeping me company but not intruding on my private time. The daughter-in-law was frantic. Dig them in, she kept saying, dig them in.

Then the rain came and after three days all trace of him was gone.

Only man I ever had. Up till that man at the B & B last week, and he doesn't count.

*

And then instead of the farm being ours and the young ones living with us, suddenly it became their farm and I was living with them.

Okay, we had talked about it. Tom working on the farm with his dad, it was only right he would inherit it. But I didn't expect it so soon. I thought that would come when we were old.

Christopher never wanted anything to do with it. His dad hammered him sometimes, hammered him silly, but he still wouldn't do any of the work. Didn't even want to drive the tractor.

He was a good man, Ian, but he never liked Christopher. Not from when he was born. And yet.

And yet.

And yet they were so alike.

But Tom never put a foot wrong.

*

They stopped me doing the farm accounts. I was trained to it. Farm secretary, freelance. One day each week on a different farm. Met Ian and stayed. I did the farm accounts, and dealt with the accountant. And filled in all the Department of Agriculture forms, and they got more and more complicated across the years. I knew enough to advise the other farmers when they got stuck.

But then they bought the computer. They thought I wouldn't be able to do it. Offensive. Of course I could. I went to a Saturday morning class at the college and I'm as computer literate as the next one, but by that time it was too late.

The daughter-in-law put all the accounts and all the farm records and all the agricultural returns, everything onto the machine and wouldn't let me near it. I tried to go in sometimes when she was at work and the child was sleeping, but you needed a password and she didn't tell me it and I wouldn't ask.

But I still had the mornings, when I rose before everybody else was up.

And one day she said I wouldn't have to look after the child so much any more. We're putting him into the nursery, she said. We want him to learn social skills. Social skills? What does that mean? The child's only nine months.

And then they said they wanted to talk. We need a consultation.

We're going to sell the farm, they said.

There wasn't any future in it. It was running at a loss and wouldn't get any better. They were going to sell the farm, and what was left after paying the bank would get Tom another business, and they would have her salary as well.

What kind of consultation was that?

Mother we have a problem can we discuss it consultation? Can you advise us with your experience consultation?

How about let's decide where to live consultation. How about let's discuss how to use the money and do what we want to do consultation. What would you like to do mother?

No. We're selling the farm take it or leave it. That kind of consultation.

It was the attraction of the big money. People wanting to put their money into property and paying huge prices.

They bought a four bedroom house on a new estate with a fancy name and three bathrooms and not enough garden ground to put up a playpen.

And me?

What had they decided to do with me?

A flat in a tenement block. Three storeys up.

I didn't have to agree.

I was a free agent.

Yes, it fulfilled the terms of Ian's Will. I should always be provided with a home.

Home!

Two poky rooms in a grotty flat up in the air. It's not even in my name. They put it in her name. For the inheritance tax, they said.

I would always have a home with Christopher. I know that. If I only knew where he is.

I couldn't get up in the morning and step outside in my dressing gown. No outside to go to. My feet walk on carpets all the time. I can't feel the rhythm of the seasons. Just the throb of next door's music vibrating through the wall. I can't hear the birds singing for there aren't any. I can't feel the sun on the top of my head. The factor pays someone to come in once a fortnight to cut the grass and put weedkiller on the gravel.

I can't see the trees. How do I know what time of year it is unless I see the trees?

So I walked.

I rose early and made a coffee and then went out. No Aga now. Central heating. Living flame gas fire. No cocoon. Nothing to cocoon myself from. Nobody bothering me. No demands. Instant coffee.

I walk out, out towards the farm and past the roadend. The house and six acres went to a merchant banker who has a pony for his children. I never met him. I stayed away from the house when they were showing people round.

I walk round and back by the main road, doing the circle.

And then round again in the afternoon.

We did the Canterbury Tales at school. In April when the showers sweet, di da di da di da and good folks meet. To go on pilgrimage.

A pilgrimage to a shrine. The shrine of my life.

The daughter-in-law said it wasn't natural. She said I was just picking at the scab. Said people were talking. So I thought, I can walk someplace else.

At the church one day the minister announced the young people were looking for sponsors for a pilgrimage they were doing to Iona. I thought, that sounds good. A good long walk.

Up the West Highland Way, turn left, go to Oban, ferry to Mull, short walk to Iona. Sixty miles altogether. Three weeks or so, at my age.

That was five and a half months ago.

Well, I haven't gone straight there, have I? I walk every day. I started by walking five miles a day to begin with through places I knew, and I could still have turned for home, but I didn't. After a while I was walking through places we'd driven through, and then it was places I didn't know. I'm up to, what, ten, eleven miles a day now. Not that I keep count. Start counting and you get into a competition with yourself. Set yourself goals. Ten miles today, twelve miles tomorrow. Fourteen the day after.

No targets. Just one step forward and further from the prison. Just walk.

Before I settle down for the night in the B & B of my choice I check over my rucksack. Spare clothes, waterproofs, spare socks, Christopher's birth certificate, the painting of poppies I did when I was twenty, my mother's photo, some marbles the boys played with when they were young, blue and purple and yellow, wrapped up in one of Ian's socks.

Silly mementoes. But all I have. All I want.

Wax my boots, wash knickers, wash hair. Shower, bed. I'm becoming a connoisseur of showers. Too hot or too cold. Too fierce or too dribbly. A good night's sleep.

Then the first coffee in the morning, lying in bed. I carry my own one person percolator, and buy fresh ground beans. I savour it, then get up to a breakfast cooked by someone else, and then walk.

I walk through glens and over moorland, but through the forests is the best. I stop off at villages, and avoid the towns. I can picnic beside rivers and this time of year I can eat brambles as I walk. In bad weather I shelter in tearooms and libraries.

No one knows where I am.

No one knows who I am.

If I'm not paying with my credit card and can use cash I've drawn from an ATM, I sometimes give the B & B a name that's not real. Miranda. Melanie. Samantha. Not plain old Jean any more. Left her behind.

They found me once. Police car draws up beside me. Very polite young man. Tried to persuade me I should think about going home. At your age, he was thinking, but didn't say it.

But I am a free citizen. I told them it was entirely my own business what I was doing, and if anyone tried to stop me I would write to my MP and my MSP and my MEP. They asked if I knew the names of all those people, like they ask people with incipient Alzheimers what day of the week it is, and who is the prime minister. I knew all the names. I know the MSP personally as well, but didn't tell the police that. I asked the constable if he knew the names of his MP etc. and he didn't answer me.

Just because you're sixty two doesn't mean your brain's gone dead.

After that I did phone Tom and the daughter-in-law a few times. They were always asking where I was. Sometimes I told them the truth. Aberdeen, Wick, Berwick. Sometimes I make it up. I don't pay much attention to where I am. What does it matter where anywhere is called?

She keeps asking why. I can't convince her there is no answer. I just do it. I just walk. I am not keeping a diary. I am not going to write my memoirs. I am not going to sit my grandchildren on my knee and tell them stories of the exciting places I have been. There is no answer to the question why.

I can hear the daughter-in-law telling people about it. She's a great one for going to meetings. Discussion groups, encounter groups, empowerment groups, healing groups, womens groups, parenting groups, childrens groups, groupie groups. My mother-in-law, she'll be telling people, she's doing this wonderful thing. Pilgrimage to Iona. Obviously felt the need for a deep spiritual experience. She's been a bit lost you know, since my father-in-law died. Really broke her up. Wouldn't accept counselling. Needs closure. She'll come back fulfilled, a better person. Might not have the stamina to walk all the way of course, at her age, but she has her bus pass.

She was wild when she found I'd let the flat. But I needed the money. The rent plus my pension is enough for me to live on. They can't touch the money. It's paid into my bank account, and they don't want the fuss of evicting the tenants. And oh, joy. No council tax, no electricity bills, no gas bills, no insurance, no cleaning.

The tenants work in an office all day, staring at computer screens. At night they come home and watch television. They're not bothered about seeing any trees.

You don't need much when you're on a pilgrimage. You just want a bed for the night, bread and cheese and pickle to eat.

This morning I found myself in Oban. It was accidental. I didn't mean to be here.

The ferry for Mull and Iona lies in the harbour, black and white with a red funnel. I stand on the quayside watching the people piling onto it. I could go there, I could buy a ticket and climb aboard and finish my journey. I could do what I told everyone I was going to do.

I could go to Iona where I've heard it said that the veil between heaven and earth is gossamer thin. I could finish my pilgrimage there. It would be a neat ending to all these months of journeying.

And then what?

And then go home?

The year has turned. The geese are flying south.

I toss the mobile phone and charger into a waste bin and watch some boys scrabble for it. I tell them they can keep it. There's still some airtime left on it. They'll try and track me through the phone. The signals will tell them where I am, or in this case, where I'm not.

I'm turning south. While the weather is still mellow I shall walk to the south coast and catch a ferry for France. South, always south, to warm seas and red wine, and black velvet nights.

If anyone asks, I can say I'm on pilgrimage.

I may come north again in the spring. I may not. I may walk the world. Nameless.

Dancing at Alice's Wedding

Tomorrow they were going to Alice's wedding, so they had to gather the eggs tonight.

It could only be done in a reasonable time if Martin helped her. After they'd eaten they went out in the dark and did two hen houses each.

The lights in the sheds were still on. They were programmed to go off at 10 o'clock. The hens had quietened for the night and her entry caused a fluttering and an outcry.

We can't fool them, she thought. They know when it's night time and when it's winter and you can give them all the artificial light you like but their body clocks tell them different.

She moved along, gathering the eggs which had rolled clear of the hens' feet into the wire catchers. She loaded them onto the plastic trays on the old pram frame that served as a trolley. Most of the hens laid during the night, and she'd already collected a full quota of eggs this morning. That, thankfully, meant there weren't quite so many now. Tomorrow night when they got back from the wedding there would be a full twenty four hours' laying to be gathered and graded.

The hens settled down again as she moved along the rows.

Tomorrow she would mix with other people, some friends, some strangers, dressed up, eating, drinking, laughing and dancing.

They would dance, country dances and modern dances. The dashing white sergeant, and waltzes, and strip the willow. That was her favourite. She could never sit down when a strip the willow was announced, but would grab the nearest man and join in. There had been some wild memorable strip the willows.

Outside, they loaded the plastic trays onto the big trolley. She did a quick calculation. Two and a half dozen eggs to a tray, six trays to each stack, and the four sheds had yielded three stacks each. A hundred and eighty dozen eggs, give or take. Martin brought out the last of his trays.

They didn't speak. Inside, the sheds had been warm. Out here the temperature had fallen since early evening. Martin was coughing again. He'd caught a bad dose of cold, but he said that was all it was.

Between them they pushed the heavy trolley along to the grading shed.

I'll do the grading, she said. You go to bed.

Sure?

Yes, sure, it's a long day tomorrow.

She stood at the door of the grading shed and watched him pick his way carefully down the track to the house. He was briefly silhouetted in the light from the kitchen and then the door closed and all was quiet again.

There were stars out and the faint sparkle of frost on the weeds which pushed through the tarmac of the yard promised a cold night.

Inside the grading shed was as cold as out. She slid the big door closed and lit the calor gas heater.

She switched on the grading machine, and it began its gentle clickety clack. She loaded the eggs into their cups on the conveyor belt. Her fingers were cold and she fumbled and dropped a couple of eggs which smashed on the cement floor.

As the sorted eggs began to pile up she left the loading and started to pack them onto the fibre trays on which Martin would take them to the market on Monday.

Her portable radio played softly, the music interrupted occasionally by the murmurings of continuity announcers. She only half listened, soothed by the gently clicking of the machine and the slight hiss of the gas in the heater beside her.

Tomorrow she would rise as usual at seven but wouldn't need to stir the stove into life. The porridge could be made on the electric cooker. Martin would get up, and after they'd eaten they would dress in their best clothes. These were already laid out in the spare bedroom. Martin's dark suit with a new white shirt and her own outfit, the faithful brown dress and jacket. It still fitted. She hadn't put on any weight for years.

They had been girls together, her and Alice. Alice would be a famous scientist and she would be an award winning investigative journalist. Except when Alice was going to be a politician, and she would be a doctor. But Alice's mother became ill and her father died so Alice gave up her job and stayed at home and that was that. And now her mother had died and Alice was going to marry, and move abroad, where she would find warmth, and love.

There was a mirror behind the travelling row of eggs. This was designed so that the operator could see any cracks in the eggs and lift them off before they tumbled from their rubber cups. A broken egg in the machine made an awful mess and meant washing the other eggs. Producers weren't supposed to do that.

She leaned forward and tipped the mirror slightly to reflect her face, tired, too many shadows, but then it was eleven o'clock at night. The murmur of the newscaster on the radio had just told her that. How could she not look tired?

She would be fine tomorrow. A little bit of make up would do it for nobody would be looking at her. It was Alice's day. And everybody would be saying how glad they were, for everybody loved Alice.

The mirror swung back on its hinges. She went round the other side of the machine and loaded up more eggs.

Her back was warm from the heater, but her feet were cold for there was little protection in the wellingtons, despite her thick socks. She stamped on the concrete floor to get some feeling back. Last winter a rug lay beside the machine to give some insulation. What had happened to it? Thrown out, probably. Too many broken eggs dropped on it, making it stink. She would find another one tomorrow. No, the day after. Tomorrow they were going to the wedding.

Toss the last of the empty trays back onto the trolley and that's the job done.

She switched the machine off and the murmur of the radio became clearer in the silence. Her shoulders were aching, but she took time to sweep up the broken eggs from the floor and put them in the covered bin.

Everything had to be turned off, double checked, fire, radio, lights. The silence was palpable.

Outside, the cold made her gasp, but the clean air was something to be savoured for a moment. As her eyes became accustomed to the dark she could make out a lot of stars. The plough had swung round to the south. The black forms of the trees stood out against the sky. Martin had left her the torch, but it was hardly needed.

She slid the heavy door closed and padlocked it.

The frost was hard now and as she stepped forward her foot slid gently on black ice.

Cautiously she picked her way down the slope towards the house. Then her feet went from under her. The torch clattered away in the darkness and went out.

She lay for a moment, winded. Her foot was twisted under her. She took some deep breaths and slowly turned herself over onto hands and knees and put her good foot on the ground. A tuft of grass gave her enough leverage to ease herself upright. There was a shooting pain through her foot when she put her weight on it.

The cold had by now penetrated to her bones. She hadn't bothered earlier to put on a hat or gloves. The square of light that was the kitchen window seemed very far away. It was no use shouting for Martin. He would be in bed asleep by now.

It occurred to her that if she had broken her leg and couldn't move she could die out here of hypothermia. Or hit her head and become unconscious. Or her spine. Or both hips.

Laughing at herself for a melodramatic fool she paused to get her footing again. The torch had disappeared in the darkness. By the time it was found in the morning the batteries would be killed by the cold.

Painfully she inched her way forward, unable to put any weight for more than a moment on the damaged foot. She wished she had a stick. The grass verge beside the tarmac of the track was uneven and painful to step onto but gave her a better footing. The cold was seeping through the rubber of her thin wellingtons. Now and again she could lean against a tree and occasionally grip a branch from the hedge. It was more an illusory support than real.

Everything was silent. This was not a night for small creatures to be out, and there was no rustling such as she sometimes heard on summer nights. The sedge is withered from the lake and no birds sing. That old ballad had been her favourite at school. She and Alice declaimed it mournfully to one another, for weeks, that year she'd had to recite it at the prizegiving.

She left the shelter of the trees. To get down the three steps that led to the kitchen door she had to sit on the ground and slide down. She pulled herself upright on the door handle and fell thankfully into the warm kitchen.

The stove had gone out but there was still some heat left in it, and she gripped the towel rail and leaned over the hotplates.

When she stopped shaking she pulled off her wellingtons. Her foot had swollen up. She held it against the door of the oven and felt the warmth through her sock.

She limped through the house, holding onto furniture to help her. From the bedroom drifted Martin's snores, the

82

noisy sound of a man with a bad head cold. He would be miserable at the wedding tomorrow.

She ran a hot bath and stripped off her clothes. There were specks of dirt embedded in her hands and little droplets of blood seeping through the scratches. Her knees were an angry red, and painful, but the skin wasn't broken.

The hot water gave a blissful relief. Her throbbing foot had swollen up. She kneaded it gently to check that nothing was broken. She soaped herself. The smell of the henhouses was permanently in her nostrils but maybe no one else would be conscious of it. She'd lived with it so long there was no way of knowing for sure.

Tears coursed silently down her face, but she was careful not to make a sound.

Martin didn't stir when she climbed in beside him and eased herself into the curve of his back. Now she became aware of an ache in one shoulder, twisted perhaps when she fell.

Tomorrow they would go to Alice's wedding. They would laugh, and make jokes, and explain themselves. And when they came back from the wedding she would change into old clothes and grade eggs again.

Mabel becomes an Anchorite

When my friend Mabel decided to be an anchorite, her husband said it was all right by him as long as she paid the £1.37 out of the housekeeping and did she realise she would have to give up the drink. She said the second bit was right enough though that was maybe a simplified way of putting it, but she was damned if she could see where the £1.37 came in.

It turned out that Phil thought an anchorite was the same as a Rechabite and his knowledge of them was confined to his Uncle Archie who paid into it for years and got quite a lot of sickness benefit back. The family said it wasn't right since it was the alcohol made Uncle Archie sick in the first place, but even his best friend couldn't accuse him of having indulged after he joined.

Anyway, I was telling you about Mabel and how she took to religion. Phil telephoned me and when I went round I found Mabel sitting there, looking out of the window with her housework not done or anything. That's not like her so I asked if she was feeling ill, and she said no, she had decided to renounce the world, that was all. She showed me a book she'd been reading and it was all about saints and martyrs, and there were these anchorites who shut themselves up in a cell and never saw a human being ever again. I've decided that's what I've been looking for, she said.

Well, I tried to be as patient with her as I could. After all, when I look at a cookery book it doesn't make me want to be a fish. There's no such thing as a twentieth century anchorite, I said. Yes there is, she said, and I'm it. I've had enough of people. I'm going to spend the rest of my life in total solitude and silence, contemplating the infinite. I said was she going into a convent and she said no, the spare bedroom. I thought about this for a while and then said in that case could I have her long blue dress with the silver sleeves and sequins down the front. It would need taking in at the waist but luckily she's the same height as me.

Phil wanted to send for the doctor or the social work department but I thought the doctor would prescribe tranquillisers and in my opinion she looked too tranquil already. Anyway, she's always been an independent person and she wouldn't like other people knowing her business. Poor Phil. I found she hadn't made him anything to eat, so I cooked him a nice cheese omelette which I always find very acceptable in emergencies, and he enjoyed it and felt much better. He had a bowling match on so he went away and I went up to the spare bedroom to have a serious talk with Mabel.

I mean, it was obvious what the trouble was. A lot of people want single beds by the time they reach Mabel's age and you don't have to make such a big thing about it. I told her this, through the keyhole, for she had locked the door, but she said I was mistaken, it wasn't like that. She just wanted nothing more to do with people. She had never liked them. The rest of her life would be spent the way she wanted it, in seclusion, and we could leave her food on the landing.

Well of course we thought she'd get over it in a day or two but she didn't. Phil thought if we didn't give her any food she would soon be hungry and come out so we tried that, but Mabel was carrying quite a bit of spare weight. She always has been very self-indulgent as this whole business shows, and it would have done her no harm to go hungry for a while. But of course the people who came to see her brought food, sometimes just an apple or a piece of cake, sometimes a boeuf en croute with asparagus, but it was enough to keep her going.

You see, word got round and people started coming. I don't know what they expected to find, or what they expected to get out of it. They sat on the landing waiting for Mabel to speak which she hardly ever did, but that didn't worry them. They would tell her their problems through the door, and sometimes she answered them and sometimes she didn't but either way they seemed quite happy.

It was nice for Phil to have company. He took the whole thing quite well, I thought. You know me, he said, Phil for philosophical. It's one of his jokes. Many a grand night we used to have at the bowling club. He was the life and soul of the party. Mabel sometimes said she wished he would get some new jokes, but then she never was one for parties, and sometimes tended to be a bit of a wet blanket after midnight, but the rest of us thought he was a laugh. We used to shout out the punchline before he came to it. It was great fun. Anyway, he was being very philosophical about Mabel's defection and I did what I could by taking his washing home.

Some Americans stopped off on their way to India. They were very interesting and not at all what you would expect by looking at them, but then they are a nation of extremes, aren't they. It was a bit of a nuisance for Phil to find nothing but goat's milk and dandelion root in the fridge when he was hungry. They sat in a circle around the house chanting, a low moaning sound. It was creepy till you got used to it. In fact you missed it when they stopped. They didn't often stop for they used to moan in relays and it was only when the moon and stars were in a certain conjunction they would stop for five minutes every hour. One of them explained it to me. It was quite exhilarating. You could hear them all the way to the by-pass.

Then there was Mr Smith from down the road. To tell you the truth I don't have much patience for people who have hobbies that make them miserable, but you have to feel sorry for Mr Smith. His spare time was spent phoning up women and breathing heavily. Of course they hung up on him immediately and it made him very frustrated. He came to see Mabel and breathed at her through the keyhole for hours and hours, and went away a happy man. He said it changed his life having a woman listen to him without interruption. He had never believed it possible. He came back several times, but he's on shift work and couldn't always manage.

The People's March for Jobs made a detour to see Mabel and stayed for a while. Their leaders stood below her window to address the crowds. Personally, I think it was mean of her not to speak to them. She'd had plenty of time to contemplate the world's problems, and come up with an answer. If she had she kept it to herself.

I was interviewed by the BBC standing under Mabel's window. I had my hair done specially and wore my green wool suit. I said it was a good thing having an anchorite in the middle of a housing scheme, for it made everybody feel more uplifted. I said the government ought to sponsor a Nun-in-Residence in every town and reduce the burden on the National Health Service. I said what's more the vandals weren't getting peace with all the people about and went somewhere else, so it was an answer to the vandalism problem as well. I've recorded the programme. I can show it to anyone who missed it.

A psychologist from the university came. He sat on the landing and asked Mabel a lot of questions about her dreams and the change of life. Of course, she didn't answer but he just sat there repeating his questions over and over again through the door. He was a persistent man, and reminded me in many ways of my late husband. We could hear Mabel humming to herself, and this made the psychologist very excited. Since she didn't answer him he started asking the people in the queue about their problems. Oh, we had some lively discussions there on the landing, I can tell you.

Poor Phil was getting a bit fed up by this time. I found him one day in the kitchen very disconsolate. The people from the women's magazine who wanted to do Mabel's life story had made an awful mess of the garden with the elevating platform they borrowed from the motorway lighting men to reach Mabel's window. Not that it did them any good for she just drew the curtains and refused to speak to them though they sat outside her window for days, but one of the wheels of the machine went over Phil's prizewinning marrow. At least it would have been prizewinning if it had survived to see the flower show. It turned out as well that all his winter jerseys were kept in the spare room and Mabel wouldn't let him in. With the weather turning a bit colder he was needing them for the bowling. That's another thing, he said. You can't get a decent game any more for everybody wanting to talk about Mabel. I comforted him for a while, and said it was my opinion that nobody could stand their own company for so long and she would soon come out.

Of course, it was inevitable that someone in higher authority would start to take an interest, so that when we saw the Royal helicopter hovering over the house I wasn't a bit surprised. I'm very sensitive to these things and I knew it was just a matter of time before Mabel received official recognition.

Well, the helicopter was hovering and looking for a place to land, and taking a while about it, for I suppose he was more used to the lawns of Buckingham Palace and the gardens round here are very small. Everybody rushed out of the house to watch him.

Except Phil. He grabbed my arm and dragged me upstairs!

But he only wanted him and me to talk to Mabel without all the people around. He pleaded with her through the door till I got fed up and I could hear the helicopter had landed, so I used my credit card to spring the lock, for it opens all doors.

And we went into the room. And she wasn't there. I was quite speechless.

Her blue dress was hanging on the wardrobe with a note pinned to it. It was addressed to Phil so I read it out to him. *Dear Phil I can't bear it. I have gone to Novaya Zemlya. Your winter woollies are in the second drawer on the right. Mabel.*

Well, I did the only thing possible in the circumstances. I mean, what would you have done? Everybody was coming, so I pushed Phil out of the room, and closed the door at our back. We waited on the landing to give the appropriate welcome.

The rest is history.

Everybody thinks Mabel's still there. It would be a shame to disillusion them, for it makes them so happy. Besides Phil's doing awfully well with the collecting boxes, and my cream teas at £4 a time have become a legend. On the other hand, I'd quite like a holiday, but I daren't leave Mabel unattended.

Still, I'm glad she left her blue dress. It fits me beautifully, after I took it in at the waist.

No Tears for Miss Chisholm

Letter from Miss Marigold Chisholm
To Mr Andrew Wentworth, MA. LLB. Solicitor, Notary Public

Dear Mr Wentworth,

I write to consult you on a legal matter.

I have done very well to have outlived my three score years and ten. My ninetieth birthday is approaching. This would be a suitable date on which to die, while I still have my health and strength. My plans are made.

However, I am burdened by possessions. My question is, is there any law against giving away everything I own?

Yours sincerely,

Marigold Chisholm (Miss)

Letter from Mr Andrew Wentworth, MA. LLB, Solicitor, Notary Public
To Miss Marigold Chisholm

Dear Miss Chisholm,

It was good to hear from you again. I am pleased you are keeping well.

I have considered carefully the proposition you outline in your letter. It is not, of course, at least not yet, illegal in this country to divest yourself of possessions.

In your particular circumstances, and knowing your financial affairs as I do, and I assume they have not changed since you were last in contact, and no doubt you would tell me if they had, potential inheritance tax is not something about which you need worry.

However, I am concerned about the other matter you raise in your letter. I wonder whether what you propose might not cause some difficulty. Perhaps we should meet to discuss this further.

Yours sincerely,

Andrew Wentworth.

Letter from Miss Marigold Chisholm
To Graham Forbes

Dear Graham,

I trust you and your wife are well. I see that you have a large and greedy car. Perhaps in your profession of upmarket bookmaker you feel this gives the right image. I disagree.

I am going to give you mine, which is small and economical. I have had many years of good service from it. I shall soon no longer have a use for it.

With best wishes,

Your aunt Marigold.

Letter from Andrew Wentworth, MA. LLB etc.
To Mr Graham Forbes

Dear Graham,

I have a client looking for a stockbroker and have recommended yourself.

However, I seize this opportunity of writing to you to raise an entirely different matter.

I have reason to believe that your aunt, Miss Marigold Chisholm, a long and valued client of this firm, is approaching her ninetieth birthday.

We in the office, that is to say myself, my partners and staff, would like to mark this occasion. I write therefore to enquire whether you know the exact date.

Please do not tell your aunt I have written to you.

Yours sincerely,

Andrew Wentworth.

E-mail from Graham Forbes
To Andrew Wentworth

Hi Andrew, Thanks for reminding me. We knew she was getting on but didn't know her age. I'll ask my wife the date. Women remember these things. Ninety's important, isn't it? Should I arrange a party? Yours, Graham.

Letter from Miss Marigold Chisholm
To The Managing Director, The National Portrait Gallery, Edinburgh

Dear Sir,

I am sending you an oil painting, artist unknown, which was made of my great uncle Herbert Chisholm, on the occasion of his retiral as second assistant chief teller with the British Linen Bank, West Nile Street Branch.

I should be obliged if you would acknowledge safe receipt.

Provided the date is not too far in the distant future, I would be happy to attend any ceremony for the installation and unveiling.

Yours faithfully,

Marigold H. Chisholm (Miss).

E-mail from Graham Forbes
To Toots@hotspot.com

Hi toots, how's the Seychelles? It's snowing here. Need some info. Had a letter from Andy Wentworth. You remember him, family solicitor since the year dot. Asking for Auntie Marigold's date of birth. Any clues? Should I buy a present just in case? Love, Giggles.

Letter from Miss Marigold Chisholm
To Mr Andrew Wentworth, MA etc.

Dear Mr Wentworth,
I am enclosing details of the running order of my funeral service. Please keep this with my Will. I have paid the undertaker.
Yours sincerely,
Marigold Chisholm.

Greetings card (Van Gogh's sunflowers) from Graham Forbes
To Miss Marigold Chisholm

Dear Aunt Marigold,
I hope you're well. We are all well. I was at an auction today and bought you a pair of candlesticks to match the cakestand you and Aunt Isabel and Aunt Marian were all so fond of. I think they are Hanoverian silver. The auction house'll deliver them to you.
With lots of love, Graham.

Letter from Miss Marigold Chisholm
To Mrs Angela Worth-Harrington

Dear Angela,
Thank you for your card. I am pleased you like the cakestand. My late sisters and I always intended that you should have it since you admired it so much every time you visited. I am sending you a pair of candlesticks. Unfortunately they are only silver plate but I know you are not a purist in these matters.
Yours in affectionate friendship,
Marigold.

E-mail from Andrew Wentworth MA etc.
To Graham Forbes

Dear Graham, I refer to my earlier letter. Are you yet in a position to advise me of the date of Miss Chisholm's birthday?
Yours sincerely,
 Andrew Wentworth.

E-mail from Graham Forbes
To Toots@hotspot.com

Hi toots, Hope you're enjoying the spa weekend. I'm a bit worried. Auntie Marigold bless her socks has sent me back the fondue set we gave her as a Christmas present in 1989. Do you remember it? That was the year everybody had them. It's never been used. What do you think this means? Is she offended? What about? What have I done? This is worrying. And when's her birthday? Old Wentworth keeps asking. Phone me between massages. Missing you. Much love, Giggles.

Note dictated by Andrew Wentworth MA etc. for Miss Chisholm's file
Attendance at Miss Chisholm's house discussing various aspects of her financial affairs. The house is looking bare. Suggested a power of attorney might be a good idea, and explained this could be used in case of heart attack stroke etc. She declined on the basis that she will not live long enough to suffer these indignities. She refused to elaborate further. Engaged 2 hours, travelling time 1 hour.

E-mail from Graham Forbes
To Andrew Wentworth

Hi Andrew, I've been to see my aunt Marigold. We couldn't have a cup of tea because she had only one cup in the house. A mug that was a present from Oban. Used to sit in the display cabinet. I remember playing with it as a boy. Has she been selling things to make ends meet? Isn't she managing on her pension? Do you think I should offer to help? I am really worried. Yours, Graham.

E-mail from Andrew Wentworth MA etc.
To Graham Forbes

Dear Graham, I have received your letter and have considered carefully its terms. Your aunt and I recently had a long and fruitful discussion on various matters. She appears to me to be very well. We can only hope that when we reach her age we all thrive as well as she does. As to your concerns, perhaps you should mention these to your aunt, who, I am sure, will be pleased to set your mind at rest. Could I remind you that you were to let me know the date of her birthday? Yours sincerely, etc.

Letter from Miss Marigold Chisholm
To Rev. Simon Fulmington, MA, DD

Dear Mr Fulmington,
I enjoyed your sermon on Sunday.
Your theme, gather not up treasures upon earth, is my own philosophy exactly. However, twenty four minutes is too short. You would benefit from more research material.
I am sending you a set of sermons by that well known preacher the Reverend Samuel Eastbrook (1827 to 1922) in fifteen volumes. They were collected by my grandfather who had an eye for a leather binding. Take care when handling

them. My cleaning lady came out in an appalling rash when she was dusting them. I've arranged for their delivery to you on Saturday afternoon, since you told me that is the day you are always at home, writing your sermon.

With very best wishes,

Yours sincerely,

Marigold H. Chisholm.

Letter from Andrew Wentworth
To Miss Marigold Chisholm

Dear Miss Chisholm,

Thank you for the utility wardrobe and the hatstand. They are fine pieces and bring back happy memories of my childhood in the aftermath of the war. However, I regret that I have to return these. The Law Society prohibits the acceptance of gifts from clients. I am sure you will understand.

Yours sincerely,

Andrew Wentworth

Greetings card (Botticelli's Venus) from Graham Forbes
To Miss Marigold Chisholm

Dear Aunt Marigold,

Got your note offering me the Singer sewing machine. My wife doesn't sew. I don't think she has time to learn. Can you send it to a Museum?

I understand Kelvingrove has hundreds of them in their basement. I expect they would like yours. But I know you'll miss it so I'm arranging for delivery to you of a new machine with all the bits and bobs for fancy work. I hope you have many happy hours of sewing in front of you.

Much love, Graham.

**Letter from Miss Marigold Chisholm
To Mr Andrew Wentworth MA etc.**

Dear Mr Wentworth,
I am sorry the Law Society will not allow you to accept gifts from clients. I am therefore sending your wife a very fine mahogany elephant, three feet high, with a lamp balanced on the end of its upraised trunk. My father brought it from India.
Yours sincerely,
Marigold Chisholm.

**E-mail from Andrew Wentworth
To Graham Forbes**
Have you found the date yet?

**E-mail from Graham Forbes
To Andrew Wentworth**
I'm trying.

**E-mail from Graham Forbes
To Toots@hotspot.com**

Hi Toots, How's Bermuda? Aunt Marigold sent round some bedclothes the other day. Do you think she thinks when you're not here I don't know how to work the washing machine? Pure silk sheets. I tried them. Slid about all over the bed. Would've been fun if you'd been here. I met her home help in the street and gave her some money so she could buy replacements for auntie. Sensible polycotton. House is empty without you. Kiss a dolphin for me. All my love, Giggles xxxxxx

Letter from Miss Marigold Chisholm
To Mr Andrew Wentworth

Dear Mr. Wentworth,
Thank you for your letter. I am very well indeed. I have ordered a coffin to be delivered tomorrow. They do a flat pack.
Yours sincerely,
Marigold Chisholm.

E-mail from Andrew Wentworth
To Graham Forbes
Dear Graham, Is it your intention, or are you aware if it is the intention of any other member of the family, or indeed friends of the family, to spend the day of Miss Chisholm's ninetieth birthday with her? Yours sincerely.

E-mail from Graham Forbes
To Andrew Wentworth
We could have a surprise party. Would you like to come? Yours Graham.

E-mail from Andrew Wentworth
To Graham Forbes
No thank you. I would suggest a surprise party might not be a good idea, at her age. Do you know the date? Yours etc. etc..

Letter from Miss Marigold Chisholm
To Graham Forbes

Dear Graham,
Thank you for your note. Please do not make any special arrangements for my birthday. I have plans of a personal nature.
Your aunt Marigold.

Letter from Andrew Wentworth
To Miss Marigold Chisholm

Dear Miss Chisholm,
Thank you for the complete sets of Sir Walter Scott, Charles
Dickens, and Annie S. Swan, good condition, slightly foxed.
My wife and I will value these.
Yours sincerely,
Andrew Wentworth

Text from Graham Forbes
To Toots
She's sent us a set of ten prints of Constable pictures,
including the Haywain. We've got some, surely.

Greetings card (puppies romping in the snow) from
Angela Worth-Harrington
To Marigold Chisholm

Darling, thank you for the eighteen pyrex casserole dishes,
some covers missing unfortunately, but still usable. Come to
dinner soon, darling.

Note from Andrew Wentworth
To the Office Cleaner
Please feel free to take away this set of gardening tools,
gifted by a kind client. Perhaps your husband can use them,
though they are slightly rusted.

Text from Graham Forbes
To Toots
And twenty two table covers with matching napkins,
embroidered by my late Aunt Isabel.

Letter from Miss Marigold Chisholm
To Mr Andrew Wentworth

Dear Mr Wentworth,
I begin to despair. At this rate I will never get to the end of things.
Yours sincerely,
Marigold Chisholm.

Letter from Mr Andrew Wentworth
To Miss Marigold Chisholm

Dear Miss Chisholm,
May I venture to suggest that the task you have set yourself is proving impossible of fulfilment because the time is not right.
Yours sincerely,
Andrew Wentworth.

Letter from Miss Marigold Chisholm
To Mr Andrew Wentworth

Dear Mr. Wentworth,
The time is right. It is the time I have chosen.
Yours sincerely,
Marigold H. Chisholm (Miss).

E-mail from Graham Forbes
To Toots@hotspot.com

Hi toots, I'd Andy Wentworth on the phone. Not clear what he was on about. The poor old thing is losing the place. Are you coming home for Aunt Marigold's birthday? Whenever it is. Missing you desperately, Giggles.

Letter from Miss Marigold Chisholm
To Mr Andrew Wentworth

Dear Mr. Wentworth,

Someone is playing a practical joke on me. Someone, unknown to me, has opened an account at John Lewis in my name and every day they deliver items I have not ordered but which I am told are paid for. Yesterday there arrived a three piece suite. In leather, Mr. Wentworth. I am a vegetarian.

How do I stop this? I suspected my nephew. Although he has made an unfortunate choice of profession, he is basically kind hearted. He denies it, and I believe him. Please find out what is going on.

Yours sincerely, Marigold Chisholm.

Letter from Andrew Wentworth
To Miss Marigold Chisholm

My dear Miss Chisholm,

This is most bewildering. I will look into it for you. There has obviously been a mistake of the type, alas, too frequent nowadays with computerisation. Please do not worry.

Yours sincerely.

Andrew Wentworth

Letter from Miss Marigold Chisholm
To Mr Andrew Wentworth

Dear Mr. Wentworth,

I have contacted the Salvation Army to come and clear my house. After that there only remains my car to be delivered to my nephew. Please send me your account for the work you have done to date.

Yours sincerely,

Marigold Chisholm.

Page 4, column 3, Daily Record

An elderly woman has been admitted to hospital following a car crash in which she was the driver. It is understood no other vehicle was involved.

E-mail from Graham Forbes
To Toots@hotspot.com

You missed the excitement. Aunt Marigold wrote off her car. Crawled out of it with just a sprained wrist. Not the one she writes with. She's going to live forever, is auntie. Set me thinking. About life and whatnot. I am being serious. I've just got you and you've just got me. Apart from auntie of course. So no nonsense. I've made up my mind. I've booked my flight. I'll be with you tomorrow. Silk sheets on the bed? XXXX and double XXXXX

Letter from Miss Marigold Chisholm
To Mr Andrew Wentworth

Dear Mr. Wentworth,

I enclose the summons which was brought to my door by two police constables. My defence is clear.

I was driving at a speed of 70 miles per hour, permissible on that road. A squirrel ran out in front of me – a red squirrel, Mr Wentworth. I had to brake. I could do nothing else. The accident was not caused by reckless driving, whatever the policeman said.

This charge is an insult. You will therefore intimate a plea of not guilty and prepare my defence. I am very angry about this. Furthermore, clearly I cannot carry out my intention of dying with this calumny hanging over me. I therefore intend to go on living until I have proved my innocence, however long that takes, and whether we have to appeal the matter to the highest court in the land.

Yours sincerely,

Marigold H. Chisholm (Miss)

Letter from Andrew Wentworth
To Miss Marigold Chisholm

My dear Miss Chisholm,

I have your letter, and agree. Such a finish to a hitherto blameless life is not to be countenanced. Your defence will be safe in my hands, no matter how long it takes.

Yours very sincerely,

 Andrew Wentworth.

Lunch with Charles

When Mrs Bannatyne woke up her first thought was to wonder who she was and where she was.

For a transcendent moment of joy she thought this must be what being dead and in heaven was like. Then everything slipped into its proper place and she was herself again. Today Charles was coming to take her out to lunch, and she did not want to go.

She would have to wash and dress up, and she had rather lost the habit of both lately.

After her shower, she chose carefully the clothes suitable for lunching with Charles. The tweed skirt in lovat green. It was now much too big for her but that could not be helped. She pulled the waist in and fastened it with a safety pin. Her turquoise blouse, and over it she would wear her black jacket. She hung this behind the front door to remind her. She fastened her pearls round her neck.

Then, because Charles would not be here for another two hours at least, she went out into the garden. She loved the garden. She cared little about the house but Charles insisted she have a woman in to clean. No one came to look after the garden.

The garden had a kiwi tree, which never bore fruit. There were three apple trees, which bore fruit of such sourness that in most years the apples fell to the ground to nourish and nurture the creatures of the earth, and eventually the earth itself.

But the pear tree – ah, that was a different story. She had planted the pear tree, and trained it against the wall, over a framework of wires and eyelets. Most of these had rusted to disintegration long ago, but enough remained, and the pear tree itself had formed its shape and knew no other, so it leaned flat against the wall, and grew every year till now it reached higher than the mossy coping stones which shed the rain down to its roots. She would go and look at the pear tree.

The paths throughout the garden were narrowing with each passing year. As she picked her way through them, her slippers soon became sodden with last night's dew. The garden was overgrown with the leggy flowers of late summer, and there drifted in the air silvery spider threads and willowherb down. She brushed against grasses and shrubs, her skirt collecting coils of bindweed and sticky billy.

She did not want to go to lunch with Charles.

She could not bear to listen to his silly chatter. Once, listening to him on the telephone talking on and on, she felt hysteria rising within her. She reached down and pulled the telephone wire from its socket. Pulled the plug, she thought with some satisfaction. Pulled the plug.

He told her later that it had taken a great deal of persuasion on his part to get the telephone people to check her line for faults. They'd found nothing wrong, and could not explain it. Mrs Bannatyne did not explain it either.

She tried not answering the phone. Twice. She stood in the kitchen listening to it ringing and did not answer it. Not on the Sunday, and again not on the Monday.

She forgot he was at Harrogate on holiday. If he had been at home he might just have driven round to see her. As it was he telephoned her local branch of the Telephone Samaritans and persuaded them to send someone to check she was all right.

When Mrs Bannatyne answered the door, the untidy young woman standing there seemed surprised, and stammered a sort of explanation. Her plump face was red, and her spectacles were misty with sweat. She had travelled by bus, and not knowing exactly where she was going, had got off the bus too early, she said. She must have walked at least a mile and half in the heat.

Mrs Bannatyne kept the girl standing on the doorstep, and when her patience gave out, shut the door. She stood at the sitting room window and watched Charles's catspaw – that was the right word, Charles's catspaw - limping down the drive.

That evening she answered the phone, knowing it would be him. Nothing was said. She would not acknowledge the incident, and neither did he.

He had been her husband's friend, not hers.

On the second anniversary of her husband's death she dressed carefully, telephoned for a taxi and went to the police station. She had never been in a police station before, and was disappointed to find how bare and quiet it was. A young man in shirt sleeves pulling on his uniform jacket came through from the back.

'Yes, madam. What can I do for you?'

'I am being stalked. I believe that is the word.'

He put her in a side room and a middle aged policewoman with a large brown mole on her face brought her a mug of milky tea which she did not want. Mrs Bannatyne explained that a man her late husband knew was pestering her, by telephoning her nearly every day, and calling at the most inconvenient times. Of course she had to let him into the house, she did not want a scene.

Was he – ah? The woman seemed to be having difficulty in framing the question. How perfectly ridiculous, thought Mrs Bannatyne. As a policewoman surely she could express herself on the unsavoury side of human nature.

He is not sexually abusive, she said, answering the question that had not been voiced.

The policewoman said no, she had been going to ask about money. Was he taking money from her? Heavens no, money was never discussed. The woman excused herself and went out. She came back with another mug of tea although Mrs Bannatyne had not touched the first one, and went away again.

Later, back home, Mrs Bannatyne pinned the policewoman's card to the cork board hanging on the kitchen wall. She found this board useful for helping her to remember things. Also, she thought, if Charles looks at it he will realise that she has been seeking advice. But he would know that anyway. The policewoman assured Mrs Bannatyne they would have a word with him.

Perhaps they did. Perhaps they did not. Mrs Bannatyne had no way of knowing. All she knew was that nothing was said, and the telephone calls from Charles continued.

She came to the pear tree and stood looking up at it. The fruit hung pale against the wall, faintly tinged pink. She reached up and plucked one. It came away easily in her hand. She turned it over and squeezed it gently with her thumb. It was ripe. She bit into it. The sweet juice ran down her chin. She picked another.

She tried to remember whether she had been having lunch with Charles on the day her husband died. No, that was wrong. It came back to her. Her husband was lunching with Charles. She had an appointment with the doctor.

Her husband hadn't believed in her illness. They had been doing tests at the hospital and he thought it was a waste of time because the illness was all in her mind.

'But if that's true it's just as frightening,' she said.

He was impatient. He told her she was just performing because she wanted attention. He used to say things like that.

But that wasn't what hurt. What hurt was that when the time of her appointment came it was only with reluctance that he drove her to the surgery.

He pulled in to the surgery car park and waited for her to get out of the car. He didn't switch off the engine.

'Aren't you coming in?'

'I'm meeting Charles.'

107

'But it might be bad news.'

'It'll be all right.'

'Don't you care?'

'Of course. But do get out, Charles will be waiting.'

He had driven off, and she stood in the car park and knew that she was going to leave him because he cared nothing for her.

Instead of going into the surgery she went home. She wrote a note, packed a suitcase and telephoned for a taxi. She caught the first train that came in to the station, and travelled to the seaside. She booked into a hotel, and went out to find a telephone.

There was a telephone kiosk outside a fish and chip shop. As she stood in it, the smell of frying and vinegar was overwhelming. She had not eaten since breakfast.

The phone rang for a while. Surely he should be back by now? It was answered suddenly.

'Hullo?'

'Charles, what are you doing there?'

'My dear.'

'What?'

'My dear, come home.'

Her husband had collapsed at the golf club and had been rushed to hospital in an ambulance. Charles was back at the house looking for her. By the time she had checked out of the hotel (they kindly did not charge her anything, once she explained) and caught the next train back, her husband was dead.

When she got home the note had gone from the kitchen table. Of course Charles had found it. Nothing was said. Not then, not since.

She finished the pear and tossed the core into the bushes. She saw that some of the juice had dribbled onto her blouse. She rummaged in her skirt pocket and found an old handkerchief. She scrubbed at the marks on her blouse but they were beginning to dry. She could not go to lunch with Charles in a dirty blouse.

She would not go. She would not lunch with Charles.

As she walked she undid the buttons on her blouse and shook it off.

She undid the clasp of her string of pearls and tossed it away from her. It landed in a holly bush, and slithered down till it caught. The diamonds in the catch glistened for a moment as it twisted and swung and then it was still.

She stepped out of her skirt, then her tights, her brassiere and her knickers.

She turned back to the pear tree and picked another. You'll spoil your lunch. She could hear her mother's voice. I know, she said aloud. But I'm not going to lunch.

She sat down, enjoying the feel of the long silky grass, and the warm stones of the wall on her skin. There was no wind here.

She must have fallen asleep, for she was woken by the crunch of car wheels, distantly, on the driveway at the front of the house. The car door slammed. She did not move. Charles could let himself in. He had a key.

After a while he appeared on the terrace. She heard him call her name. From where he stood he could not see her, sitting on the ground by the wall, by the pear tree. He went back into the house. He would be searching. He would come out into the garden, but not too soon, for he hated to get his shoes dusty or muddy. It would take some time.

She reached up and plucked another pear.

At the Tip

As there was no one else to do it, Anna cleared the house after her father died. On her mother's death her father refused to let her do anything to help. He told her he had taken the clothes to the charity shop. Now, five years later, she found he had lied.

It took her two weeks. Each day she spent several hours in the house, sorting systematically through drawers and wardrobes and cupboards.

Each evening she went back to her own flat, giving herself a good shake on the mat, undressed completely in front of the washing machine and dropped her clothes into it, washing her hair and showering before she had her meal.

Each morning she went back to the house, threw open all the windows again to clear the sour smell, and continued sorting and sifting. She set aside the things which the auctioneer's man had suggested would sell, and stuffed bin bags full of rubbish. She packed the wheelie bin, then the bins of neighbours, who wouldn't, she knew, dare say anything. Bereavement was a useful shield. One of the bags she stacked against the bin was torn open by a dog and then attacked by seagulls and the contents strewn over the pavement. No matter, the bin men would clean it up.

Sheets turned side to middle, towels worn thin with use, lumpy cushions in stained satin covers, all these were stuffed into bags and dumped outside.

She filled two bags with crockery, a lot of it chipped and cracked. As she upturned the cutlery drawer into the bag a memory came back to her of her mother during one of her illnesses, when she needed nursing. Anna had been able to wash the shit of her incontinence off her without concern, but sitting in the kitchen with her father eating, these grey metal forks had turned her stomach.

There seemed to be no end of stuff. Where on earth had they found such hideous ornaments. Why keep so many broken bits of electrical equipment, so many gadgets that even when they were new and working were probably more bother to clean than they were worth. There were papers everywhere, old letters, receipts, guarantees for equipment long since defunct. She stuffed them into bags, not bothering to sort through them. There was nothing an identity thief could use.

Her mother's wedding dress was in a cardboard box at the foot of the wardrobe. She pulled out the box, and unwrapped the brown paper tied with string. Underneath she found layers of tissue paper and there it was. A photograph of her mother in this dress stood on the sideboard for years. When her father died, the photograph was on his bedside table. It was made of creamy satin, with ruffles. It must have been difficult to come by just after the war. Anna examined it closely. The stitching had all been done by hand. Had her mother made it, with the help of her sisters? Or perhaps they could afford to pay someone to do it.

She could have laughed. All that effort, working against time too, for her mother had been pregnant when she wore this. When she was twelve Anna accidentally saw her birth certificate and before her mother could hide it again she had seen enough to work out that she was a six months baby, common enough, presumably, at the time. Later of course she needed the birth certificate and her mother gave her one of the abbreviated ones, that didn't show details of parents. Did people still get those now? Now that nobody bothered?

At twelve years old, devastated by the knowledge that she was the cause of her parents' marriage, that it was her fault these two unlikely people had to live together, she watched them carefully for a long time, looking for any sign of passion or abandonment. Now, she could look back at the timid adolescent she had been and be thankful she grew up

111

in such a quiet home. They'd learned their lesson. Who could say when enthusiasm might explode into passion and lead to perdition?

Don't eat that you won't like it. Don't spend your pocket money on lipstick. Don't think you're better than anyone else. Don't sit there dreaming. Don't cause trouble. Don't, don't, don't.

She set the dress to one side. It was old enough to be interesting. Perhaps the auctioneers would be able to sell it to a collector.

Another drawer was packed carefully with things still in their wrappings. There were pillowcases wrapped in cellophane, table napkins in a box, a tablecover made of Irish lace, spotted brown where the pins were rusted. There were cards with them. These were wedding presents which had never been used.

She opened a flat box and eased back the tissue paper. It contained a mirror, a small one with a long mother of pearl handle. She picked it up and looked at it. It was as good as new.

She remembered the old films she had seen; the films where the heroine would sit at a dressing table and lift a hand mirror and look at herself in it, turning her head this way and that, stroking her hair, smiling secret thoughts. Hidden, of course, from the hero, but not from the enchanted audience in the dark cinema.

She looked at her reflected face, so like her mother's. This was an odd present to give a couple marrying. There was a card underneath. She read it. To my love. Just that. *To my love*. Presumably a present from her father to her mother. On their wedding day perhaps?

Kept in its box. Unused? Or to protect it from herself as a clumsy child?

The unused wedding presents she set aside for the auctioneer. She hesitated over this mirror. But no, she had made her decision and she would stick to it. None of this stuff would go to her flat. The mirror was laid aside with the rest.

She found photographs in one of the drawers in the sideboard. For a moment she paused, lifting them and letting them sift through her fingers. There weren't many. There were very few of her as a child. Her parents weren't the sentimental type to have a record of her growth across the years. The only camera she remembered was a box brownie, long lost. There were some school photos. Those could certainly go out. In fact they could all go out. What use had she for a record of the past?

Emotion without action is self-indulgence, her mother used to say. Getting sentimental over some old photographs had no purpose. Why should she keep them? She'd no children to pass them on to. Get rid of them. She couldn't put them out to the bin. It would be nearly a week before the bin men came back and they might be scattered over the road. It wasn't nice to think of other people handling them. She would take these direct to the tip herself. She fetched a fresh bin bag and emptied the drawer into it.

In the boxroom she found the toys which she had played with as a child, packed away in two cardboard boxes which fell apart as she handled them. She could understand them keeping the photos. That was what photos were for, but a child's toys? She turned them over in her hands. There was a china faced doll and she set it aside, for it was probably worth something. There was a teddy bear, very worn. There were several books, Enid Blyton, Heidi, the Chalet School. Some of them were scribbled over. Oh yes, she remembered those all right. She desired fervently to be part of a gang, to be part of a family. She craved a brother, pestered her parents for a brother. Don't want what you can't have. The toy blackboard had woodworm.

She heaved the bags into the boot of the car and locked the front door behind her for the last time. Everything left would be cleared by the auctioneers, who, their man had assured her, would leave it swept and clean. She need never go back.

The tip was five miles away. She sang as she drove. Her voice felt cracky. The last time she sang had been at the funeral. Her father seemed to take some mild pleasure in the last few weeks of his life working out the order of service and had chosen the hymns. Emotion without action is self-indulgence, and what kind of emotion might you give way to when you were dying, if you didn't keep a tight grip?

What a nonsense funerals were. She'd felt impatient with the minister for his death-denying euphemisms. They diminished her father. Her father was matter of fact when faced with his imminent death, just as he had been unemotional after his wife died. Shock, people said then, but Anna knew better.

Grief is the eighth deadly sin.

The day was hot and she drove with the window down, enjoying the breeze on her face. She thought of her cool white flat, which would never be contaminated with the detritus of her parents' lives.

At the tip she drove up onto the narrow ramp alongside the skips. There was a car in front of her with a trailer. She pulled the sacks out and dropped them one by one into the skip nearest.

Anna climbed back into her car. She would have to be patient for the trailer in front was full and the driver was taking his time to offload the stuff.

The attendant came over and helped shovel a lot of garden rubbish out of the trailer.

In her wing mirror she saw the two tinkers wandering along the ramp at her back. They were dressed no different from anyone else, the woman in a blue fleece and polyester trousers and the man in jeans, but the clothes were filthy, and their skins were dingy and their hair matted. They went straight to her skip and tore open the bags she'd dropped in.

Oh don't, she cried to herself, please don't. But she sat unmoving, not turning her head, watching them in her wing mirror. The stuff didn't belong to her now. It didn't belong to anyone. It was rubbish. The woman took the teddy bear from the bag and looked at it, and pushed it inside her fleece. She pulled out the books and examined them and tossed them into the skip.

Anna started up the engine with the intention of reversing out, but a van had come up at her back and was unloading some lengths of timber. As she watched, a child tumbled out of the van and began picking out little bits of wood from the back of the van and dropped them into the end skip, laughing at the noise they made as they slipped down the metal, setting up a clanging echo.

The woman found the photographs. She said something to the man who took them from her, spilling them through his hands. Then, with a shrug he tossed them aside. He threw the blackboard to the back of the skip. Anna could hear the crack as it hit the side and broke up. She put her head on her hands where they rested on the steering wheel and moaned gently.

There was a toot behind her. She started and looked in her rear view mirror. The people at her back were finished, and the car in front was moving off. She started her engine and engaged first gear and drove off the ramp.

Two Nuns Calling

'The nuns came again today,' Miss MacCall broke the silence as she came through from the kitchen with the teapot.

Anita didn't want tea, and she had doubts about the cleanliness of the cups, but allowing the old lady to make the tea had filled some of the time.

'Are they not coming quite a lot?' she asked.

'That's the second time this week.' There was pleasure in her voice.

'I thought you went to the Church of Scotland.'

Miss MacCall straightened the saucers and cups and teaspoons and filled a plate with biscuits out of the tin Anita had given her last Christmas.

'I am a daughter of the manse,' she said. 'But my father preached tolerance. He came through the Great War. He served with distinction. He always afterwards held the view that closed minds cause wars.'

The flat was on the top floor and the June sun was hot through the bay window. From where Anita sat she could see the roofs of the tenements opposite, and beyond that the roofs of the tenements in the next street. These were good solid buildings. They had stood for a hundred years and would stand for another hundred. She and Alan had stretched themselves to buy the flat on the ground floor, but it would be worth it, a good investment. It wasn't as bright as this one but on the other hand, she wouldn't want to climb four flights of stairs after a day's work.

The grandmother clock beside the fireplace chimed four light sweet notes. The mahogany casing had a patina from decades of polishing. It must be worth a fair bit.

'That's a beautiful clock,' said Anita.

'It was a wedding present to my mother,' said Miss MacCall. 'It came to me after my father died and their home was sold. That was what brought me back from Italy, the death of my father. I have been thinking a lot about Italy recently. Sister Adrienne, one of the nuns who call regularly, she has lived there too. At a different time from me, of course. She is many years younger. They have a sister house in Assisi. I remember it well. I was there just after the war. I should have gone back. I liked it there. I liked it very much.'

She lifted her face to the sun and smiled.

'It must be nice to be a nun,' said Anita. 'Not have to do anything. Just pray, isn't that what they do?'

'Goodness me, they work as hard as anybody. Their order have a care home here for the elderly. I intend to visit it soon. I will be making arrangements. They have a place for me. I think I am beginning to look forward to it. I find the company of the religious very congenial. We had many contacts with them in Italy. We worked in a village in the mountains near Assisi, helping refugees after the war. In the evenings after work I would run down to their chapel and sit through vespers. It was a tranquil place. There was a serenity there I have never found anywhere else.'

'Weren't you tempted to become a Catholic?'

'No, no my dear. I couldn't do that. I visited Rome once, but I was brought up, after all, in an austere tradition, and it didn't take. Besides, it would have hurt my father. But much as my loyalty has always been to the Church of Scotland, you could not call it serene. My brother's children left the church, you know. They were a rebellious generation. You young people nowadays are much more conventional. You do not question, you seem to have nothing to kick against. You are the poorer for it.'

Anita was beginning to feel sleepy in the sun. She really ought to make a move to go. Alan was at the gym and wouldn't be home for a while, but she felt she had done her duty by Miss MacCall for this week.

'Is there anything you need, anything I can get you from the shops?'

'No, thank you my dear,' said Miss MacCall.

*

'She's getting a bit odd in her ideas,' Anita told her husband as she dished the asparagus.

'No business of ours. I don't know why you bother visiting her anyway,' said her husband, who was opening the Chardonnay.

'It's good neighbourliness,' said Anita. 'We have to keep an eye on the elderly.' She placed some curls of butter on the vegetables. 'Hypothermia, things like that.'

'Is her house cold?'

'Of course not. Not at this time of year,' said Anita. 'But it's not very clean.'

*

She met Miss MacCall soon after they moved in. Miss MacCall had been ahead of her, carrying her groceries in a rucksack on her back. The old soul was quite bent over with the weight of it and Anita hurried to take it and carry it up the stairs. Imagine. She'd lived on the top floor for over thirty years and still climbed the sixty two stairs practically every day.

Since then she made a point of visiting Miss MacCall regularly in case there was anything she wanted. Miss MacCall would not admit to having a need for anything, but just visiting was a help. Old people need reassurance there's someone there for them.

*

In November Miss MacCall became ill.

She collapsed in the close one Saturday morning. Fortunately Anita heard the clatter and came to investigate. Two of the neighbours carried Miss MacCall up to her flat, and sent for the doctor. He came and scolded her for not coming to the surgery for her flu injection, and recommended rest and paracetamol.

*

'It was lucky you were there,' said Miss MacCall's niece, over Miss MacCall's bed. 'She might have lain for hours otherwise.'

'Not really.' Anita had to be honest. 'Not on a Saturday morning. There are plenty of people about.'

'Still.' Mrs Grimble smiled down at Miss MacCall. 'I was just saying how lucky you were Anita was there, auntie.'

'I heard you,' said Miss MacCall. 'It's flu I've got, not deafness. Nor senility.'

'They should organise a home help for you. At your age,' said Mrs Grimble. 'You won't be able to look after yourself for a while.'

'Rubbish. It's easy to boil an egg, you know,' said Miss MacCall. She closed her eyes.

'She's getting tired,' whispered Anita.

Mrs Grimble nodded. 'I'll just push off, auntie.'

'Goodbye,' said Miss MacCall, without opening her eyes.

'It's a bit of a trail from the south side,' Mrs Grimble said to Anita at the door.

'I'll keep an eye on her,' said Anita. 'No need to worry.'

'They're tough, that generation.'

After Mrs Grimble left Anita went round the house to check everything was all right. She opened all the windows to give the place a good airing. She found a cloth in the kitchen and ran it over the surfaces, causing little eddies of dust which caught in her nostrils. She rubbed the cloth over the grandmother clock.

119

She stood on the threshold of the bedroom, listening to Miss McCall's quiet breathing. She was asleep.

The bareness of the bedroom struck her. It was painted cream, or maybe white which had become discoloured over the years. There was only the single bed, a chest of drawers and a wardrobe. I hope I never buy a single bed, thought Anita. That would really be giving up. The only decoration was a painting which hung on the wall opposite the bed, a watercolour of pink houses with orange tiled roofs and mountains in the distance. Italy, perhaps. She closed the door gently so as not to waken the old lady.

In the kitchen she set to and washed up all the dirty dishes, carefully, for some of the pretty china was obviously old. Putting it away she took the chance to rearrange the contents of the cupboard in a more logical way. The old soul obviously couldn't be bothered keeping it tidy.

Next, the fridge. She took everything out and tipped most of it into a bin bag. Too much of it had half price stickers on. Perhaps she only had her pension, and could only afford to buy food that was up to its sell by date. False economy. You could poison yourself that way. She set the fridge to defrost. She would come up later and wash it out.

As she sat back on her heels, satisfied, she heard a noise and looked up to see Miss MacCall standing in the kitchen doorway.

'There,' said Anita. 'All tidy now, but you shouldn't be out of bed.'

Miss MaCall's lips twitched and she slid gently to the floor.

The doctor came again and sent for an ambulance.

'A stroke,' said Anita to Mrs Grimble on the telephone. 'She must have been weakened by the flu. She's in the Western Infirmary.'

'Does she want to see me?'

'Don't think so. She's asking for the nuns. She hasn't said about anybody else.'

'Nuns?'

Anita told Mrs Grimble about the nuns.

*

After they visited Miss MacCall in the hospital, Anita took Mrs Grimble to a coffee shop in Byres Road.

'Are they real nuns?' asked Mrs Grimble when she had settled herself.

'What?'

Mrs Grimble picked up the menu and signalled to the waitress. 'The nuns that visit auntie, they've obviously made a strong impression on her. But are they real?'

'You mean, they might be confidence tricksters. Trying to get money out of her, or intending to steal something. A disguise to take advantage of old people. That's despicable.'

'No, no. You're not understanding me. I mean, do they really exist? I think they're a figment of auntie's imagination.'

Anita hadn't thought of that. Their coffee and cakes came while she pondered Mrs Grimble's suggestion.

'Well, I must say, she's been talking about them for a while, but I've never seen them myself.'

'Exactly,' said Mrs Grimble. 'Has anyone seen them? She's getting very old you know. She's probably getting wandered. Living alone does funny things to people.' She pressed her fork into her meringue, bursting it into a cloud of white dust.

*

Miss MacCall was making a good recovery. As the doctor said, she was fundamentally very strong for her age. All those stairs kept her fit. But it was obvious she was anxious about the future.

121

'I would like to go into the home the nuns run,' she told Anita. 'I would like them to come and see me to make arrangements. There is no reason for me to be in hospital.'

'Well, you're being looked after here.' Anita looked round the small ward. It only held four beds. The other three beds were also occupied by old ladies. There were worse places. They even had a television set, which Miss MacCall didn't have at home. Big Ben clanged six and the news came on.

'It's the noise,' said Miss MacCall. 'Please contact the nuns and ask them to come and see me.'

'I'll look out for them,' she promised, and then, remembering what Mrs Grimble had said, she asked 'What do they look like?'

'Like nuns,' said Miss MacCall, as sharply as Anita had ever heard her speak, though her voice was not strong now. 'They wear long black dresses with veils and wimples.'

'Any nuns I've seen around don't dress like that. They wear ordinary clothes. They let their hair grow. I've even seen some wearing lipstick.'

'Those aren't my nuns,' said Miss MacCall.

*

'I think you must be right,' said Anita on the telephone to Mrs Grimble.

'I told you, it's all in her mind. She's remembering the nuns she knew in Italy.'

'Was she really in Italy?'

'Oh yes, after the war. Looking after refugees. We got quite bored listening to my father going on about auntie's exploits. Quite the heroine.'

*

'I wish to go and live with the nuns,' said Miss MacCall. 'They have promised me I can go there.'

'Where is this, auntie?' asked Mrs Grimble.

Miss MacCall looked round the ward. She seemed to Anita to be more frail, and her speech was not as clear as it had been.

They waited in silence.

'I don't remember,' said Miss MacCall.

'Are you thinking about the nuns in Italy?' asked Anita gently.

Miss MacCall closed her eyes and murmured something.

'Speak up auntie. I can't hear you.'

'I don't remember.'

*

'I'm arranging to take her to live with me,' said Mrs Grimble on the telephone to Anita. 'Nobody belonging to me is going into a care home.'

'I wouldn't like her to go into a home,' agreed Anita. 'You hear stories.'

'And they're expensive. Her house would have to be sold to pay for it.'

'Would the nuns charge as much?'

She could hear Mrs Grimble drawing in her breath. 'The nuns are a figment of auntie's imagination. They do not exist.' She enunciated each word slowly, as if speaking to an imbecile.

'Of course not,' said Anita. 'So they don't.'

*

Anita went one day to visit Miss MacCall at the house of her niece.

The grandmother clock was standing in the hall, and Anita remarked on it.

123

'It's a family heirloom,' said Mrs Grimble. 'My daughters are quarrelling over it already. It's stopped, which is a nuisance. Maybe moving it has affected the workings.'

Miss MacCall was in bed.

'What a pretty room,' said Anita, admiring the matching curtains and duvet cover smothered in roses, the china shepherdesses on the mantelpiece and windowsill.

She has failed sadly, Anita thought. She was thinner and her speech was slurred.

'You remember me, Miss MacCall,' she asked.

Miss MacCall looked at her for a long time.

'Is my house all right?'

'Yes,' said Anita.

This was a lie. Miss MacCall's house had been sold, for a sum that caused the neighbouring owners to draw in their breath with delight. Miss MacCall must have forgotten. Perhaps Mrs Grimble had a power of attorney and would have dealt with all the legalities to save Miss MacCall the worry.

'Have you seen the nuns?'

'No. They've not been round.'

'If they come, will you send them to me?'

Anita nodded. 'Of course I will.'

'I trust you. You have been kind to me. You will speak to the nuns?'

'I promise.'

'Thank you. I must make arrangements to live with them.'

'It's sad,' she said to Alan that night. 'She's very wandered.'

*

Miss MacCall died a few months later. Anita took the morning off work and attended the funeral.

Walking out of the graveyard afterwards she said to Mrs Grimble. 'The last time I saw her she was still talking about nuns.'

'Oh them,' said Mrs Grimble. 'Yes, they came to the door. Don't ask me how they found out where she was. Probably got it from one of her nosy neighbours. I sent them packing. There was no need for them to see her. She wasn't one of them.'

Furniture

Sarah went into her bedroom one afternoon to find all her clothes on the floor. She hung them back in the wardrobe.

Downstairs in the kitchen she collected all the rubbish which was strewn about the floor and put it into the dustbin.

Then she sat down outside and waited.

When she went back in the contents of the bin were once more all over the floor, and upstairs her clothes were lying in a heap.

After some more thought she went along to visit the parish church minister. He declined to do an exorcism, being a modern man who didn't believe in such things. He agreed however that the rebellious furniture could be included in the next jumble sale.

The wardrobe was sold to a family who believed in simplicity and non-attachment, and for whom an empty wardrobe was a delight. The dustbin went to a couple who recycled everything anyway.

Sarah prefers not to talk about the experience.

In the Park

I'm waiting for my husband. I've seen you before haven't I. You'll have seen us. I come here every day. He'll get here at five past one. I use this bench because I can see the top of his bus when it draws up at the bus stop by the gate.

Every day.

He brings the sandwiches. You'll have noticed him, carrying a rucksack.

What do you do? Nice. We have a computer in the shop. Well a computerised till. Everything coded. Different kinds of dry cleaning. People don't realise how complicated it is. Different treatments you can give different fabrics. Brocades, velvets, that sort of thing. We get a lot of good quality cleaning in my shop. It's quite a wealthy area this, isn't it. Wedding dresses. It's surprising how dirty wedding dresses get. Mud round the hem. Dusty in summer. Sometimes there's wine spilt, and the smell of cigarettes. They come across here to get the photos taken. Little burrs on. You know? The green sticky things. When I was wee we called them sticky willy.

I leave him the stuff to make up the sandwiches so that he can choose what we have. Cheese, corned beef, chicken sometimes, salady stuff, chutney, mayonnaise. Not egg. I don't like egg. If it was left to him we'd have egg every day. He'd boil up a dozen at once and then just use one or two a day till they were finished. He says they would keep for weeks, cooked, but I don't believe that. I've never liked the smell of eggs so I don't have them in the house.

When he started being ill I was at my wits end. The doctor said it was depression and gave him medication.

He wanted me to stay at home, take time off, but I couldn't do that. I couldn't give up my job. Well, the reason for the depression was that he'd been made redundant, so it's as well one of us is working.

And I'd just been made manager. The company weren't going to tolerate a manager being off all the time.

The trouble living in a house with someone suffering from depression is that you don't know what you're going home to at night. Sometimes he'd still be lying in bed from the morning, and wouldn't have had anything to eat. At least that wasn't too bad. If he'd been lying in bed all day he couldn't be doing anything to harm himself.

Once I went home and found him sitting in the kitchen with a shotgun on his knee. I don't know where he got it and I don't want to know. I've hidden it. I don't know what to do with it.

The doctor said keeping to a routine was best so I hit on this idea of him coming to the park to meet me every day.

I had to force him at first. But he was pathetic in those days. Easy to persuade. No mind of his own. It was a symptom of the illness. I could make him do anything I wanted. I say it was what I wanted but of course it was all aimed at getting him better.

I said that if he didn't meet me in the park so that I knew where he was for part of the day, then I would have to make him go to the Day Centre. They'd make him be sociable there.

He sits where you're sitting now and doesn't say much, but we eat the sandwiches and drink a cup of coffee out of the flask, which to be honest is horrible but you can't criticise for he'll take it wrongly. And then when the hour is up I put him back on the bus and see him safe off before I return to the shop.

He complains about the bus journey. Hour and ten minutes. Then an hour with me. I only get an hour off for my lunch. My assistant minds the shop while I'm out. She has her lunch twelve to one.

Then an hour and ten minutes back. So that's three hours twenty minutes every day I know where he is.

Are you married? What d'you mean sort of. Don't be coy. Oh I see. A partner. But it's all the same isn't it. If he was ill you wouldn't leave him. Makes no odds if you've a bit of paper or not.

We met here as it happens, in this park. In the greenhouse. I was with my best friend and he was on his own. We were looking at the orchids, I remember. I've never liked orchids. You know they don't have roots of their own? They ride piggyback on other plants.

That's why it seemed a good idea to meet here. Happy memories. And handy for the shop of course.

If it's raining or cold we sit in the greenhouse. It's like an oven in there. Lovely in winter. Like the jungle must be. Hot and steamy. Expect a tiger to come out of the undergrowth.

A man I once knew gave them a plant for the greenhouse. You can do that. If you've got something unusual they don't have you can give it to them. They plant it in the glasshouse and put a little metal plaque beside it. Gifted by so and so. Of course it would have to be something very unusual. I expect they've got most things.

When I go in I always look for my friend's plant. I can never remember the name. Begins with a C. The plant I mean. Of course I remember my friend. He's dead now. The plant's still there.

I used to leave him things to do in the house, to keep him busy when I wasn't there. Things like cleaning out the grate and setting the fire ready to be lit when I got home, wash up the breakfast dishes, peel the potatoes for the dinner. Simple things like that. Well, the doctor said to keep him busy. Take his mind off himself.

He mostly did what I wanted. If he didn't I would act reproachful and sorrowful and that would make him feel guilty, so after a while he learned to do what I asked him to do.

No, I don't spend an hour and ten minutes travelling. I take the underground.

He won't travel on the underground. He hasn't since the IRA bombings in London. I know that was a long time ago, but he never really felt safe again and now there's the new terrorists aren't there, so maybe he's right.

And he feels trapped in the train, not able to get out between stations. In the bus he can say to the driver to stop and let him off. Not that he ever does. He wouldn't feel safe just wandering about somewhere. He would get into a panic.

The bus hasn't come yet. Ten past. It's late. It's happened before. I don't worry too much about it. Time enough to worry if the bus comes in and he's not on it.

He's only been late the once. The bus driver asked him to leave the bus. I don't know if that's legal, do you? I mean, he'd paid his fare, he was entitled to be taken where he wanted to go. But the bus driver said he was upsetting the other passengers and asked him to leave. Stopped the bus and wouldn't move until my husband got off.

In the end he did get off. I said he should have insisted on his rights. But he doesn't. He's not that kind of a man.

So he got off and walked here. It was about two miles away so I was pretty frantic when he arrived, I can tell you. But we ate our sandwiches. I saw him safe onto the bus for home. We had to let two buses go past because he said that might be the driver that put him off, but he agreed to go on a bus where it was a woman driving. When I got back to the shop I told my assistant I'd had a fainting fit and had been resting at the first aid station here in the park to account for being so late.

And then there was one day a difficult customer delayed me at the shop, a dress pulled a bit out of shape but we have a card in the window says we cannot guarantee success for unusual materials. I mean what do people expect if the dress was that valuable she should have gone to a specialist cleaner.

Sorry, I'm getting away from my story. So by the time I got rid of the customer it was quarter past one when I arrived here.

I was in a terrible state. You can imagine. I ran up the road like the hounds of hell were after me for I couldn't imagine what would happen when he turned up and found me not there. It had never happened before.

I could see from the gate he wasn't on the bench. And I became frantic and started searching for him all over. In the glasshouses, in the toilets, in the tearoom. I ran from one end of the park to the other.

I could feel the adrenalin, you know? My heart was pounding and the sweat was blinding me.

Then when I came back to the bench here he was eating his sandwiches. And he looked at me and he said don't do that to me again. He was totally calm.

He wouldn't tell me what he had been doing while I was looking all over for him. Hiding? Why would he do that?

But after that I made sure not to be late again. Touch wood, it didn't happen again.

Last September when the weather became colder he wanted to stop coming.

But I couldn't take the risk. I mean, he looked better and sounded better. But I thought it was safer just to keep to the routine.

He grumbled a bit, but he did as I said.

And then he started to get better. March it would be. The doctor said the medication was working. Whatever it was, I was just so glad. He was just like he was before, and taking an interest in things again.

So I thought we could stop coming here. I wasn't going to stop it dead, nothing like that. That would be too much of a sudden change. No, I thought we could tail it off gradually. You know, maybe not meet one day in the week. A Friday say. Friday I could go into town and maybe have a look round the shops.

Then after a few weeks maybe drop another day. And so on. You see what I mean? Until we were only meeting one day a week.

Then it would be a pleasure again.

He's off the medication completely now. He's perfectly well, his old self again.

Except he won't stop coming to the park.

I said to him that maybe he didn't need to come any more because he didn't need to see me and I didn't need to see him to know he was all right.

But no, he insisted. He likes coming to the park. He sees no reason why we should change our routine. So he keeps on coming. Every day.

I said to him once I won't be at the park tomorrow I'd other things I want to do. What things, he asked. Just things, I said. End of year stuff in the shop. I'll work through my lunch hour.

He came to the shop. He came storming in and started shouting for me. He created a scene in front of the customers and frightened the girl. He came through to the back shop and made me follow him out. I couldn't allow such a scene in the shop so I went with him.

I'd left my sandwiches in the shop but he had enough for both of us as usual in his rucksack and we ate them as if nothing had happened.

After that I didn't dare to argue with him.

When I go home at night he's cheerful. He keeps himself busy. I don't know what he does in the morning before he comes here, or in the afternoon after he leaves me. His time is his own and he can go and enjoy himself.

Sometimes I think it would be nice not to be here every day. It would be nice to be able to go the Art Gallery for instance, maybe in my lunch hour and look at the pictures.

Or just sit in the back shop with a book for an hour. Something.

That's his bus now.

And there he is.

Jellyfish

Down on the beach Peter was scooping up stranded jellyfish in a broken pizza tray, and running, splay legged and crouched, down to the sea with them.

Pointless. There were hundreds of the things stranded, and besides, the tide was going out.

I let myself down from the seawall and scrunched over the sand to him.

'You only have to look at them to see they're dead.'

He peered sideways at me. 'You have to try.'

He went on scooping, running, slid them into the water, came back for more.

There were so many discarded pizza trays on the beach he could have given each jellyfish its own and floated them out on the tide.

My sister was married to him. She's dead now, rest her soul, but I keep an eye.

In the Harbour Café he had Earl Grey tea, no milk, no sugar. I had a double strength cappuccino and two croissants.

Then the church bells began to ring and it was time for Peter to go to work.

That was the day the woman Heather came to church for the first time.

Peter always had more authority in the pulpit, something to do with the gown and the tabs. His neck looks less scrawny when he's wearing the tabs, instead of the collar.

Maybe it's because the pulpit is so high we have to look up at him.

He's become more serious since my sister died. I was in the church before him, as usual, playing the intro, while Peter was in the vestry. Today he'd asked for Handel's Largo. This was a bad sign. It was his privilege to choose

134

the music, but that's what he chose when he was feeling depressed.

Most women, when bereaved, and after a decent interval, blossom. Most men wither. My sister knew this too, which was why before she died she asked me to look after him.

He always was too intense. You couldn't be flippant with him. A casual remark would be studied and examined from every angle. What do you mean, he would ask.

It was bad enough in private but at parties it was grim. Social conversation would have moved on while Peter was still pondering a chance remark, a light observation, a flippancy tossed away like a stone skimming the water. Everybody else would be talking about something else by now, but Peter would dive in after it, worrying at it.

That day he'd asked me to play Handel's Largo for the intro and that was a bad sign.

After the service I played everybody out and then went down to the church door to meet Peter and found him talking to the new woman. He introduced us. Heather, she was called. Bouncy blonde curls, spiky highlights. Hours at the hairdresser, to say nothing of the money.

I walked part of the way home with her. She'd just moved to the town, and had opened a keep fit studio. Clearly, our paths wouldn't cross very often, but I'd noticed the caressing way her hand rested in Peter's when she'd said goodbye to him. I thought, better keep an eye here.

She joined the choir.

We met every Thursday evening for choir practice in the manse where I train them as best I can given the material I have to work with. I don't sing myself. I have no voice. We're six woman – seven when Heather joined – and one man, very loyal bless him, who's not quite baritone and not quite tenor, but does what he can.

Peter usually sat in on the practice, for when the church attendance is light he has to sing to make up for the dearth.

135

Heather had a loud voice, and she could hold the tune, so she became an acceptable member of the choir. She laughed a lot.

From where I sat at the piano I would often catch a glimpse of Peter's puzzled smile, as he tried to be polite in the face of her jocularity. Our choir practice took on a tone which wasn't there before, an unsettling levity.

One evening a few months after Heather came to the town, I took a meal round to the manse to share with Peter, as I often did. On this occasion it was steak and kidney pudding followed by apple pie. He was pottering about in the garden and I went into the kitchen to heat up the food, taking the chance while I was there to tidy up his cupboards a bit. I tossed out a couple of packets of food that were past their sell by date.

I was looking in the drawer for a fresh bin bag when I came across the membership card for Heather's Keep Fit Studio.

After we'd eaten we sat in the garden, for it was a warm evening. We sat, companionably, talking of my sister until it was dark, and we watched the bats flit round the manse.

He never so much as mentioned the words Keep Fit.

Soon after, I saw the two of them jogging along the beach.

I invited Heather to meet me at the Harbour Cafe.

I watched her running along the beach towards the cafe, kicking up little spurts of sand with her heels. She was a scrawny woman, much too thin for her own good. Her skin was red with wind-weathering, and her stripy hair was matted with sweat.

'Business all right?'

'Business fine,' she panted.

'You've made a great go of it. Everybody's very surprised. This isn't the kind of town that goes in for that sort of thing.'

She ordered a black coffee and I had my usual.

'Do you think it right to encourage older men to overstretch themselves?' I asked her.

'No,' she said.

'You know, heart attack, stroke, tearing worn ligaments, weakening the walls of the blood vessels, putting strain on the internal organs, hernias.'

'Most people have the sense to know when to stop. Anyway, what care do you take of his health? Overfeeding him and encouraging him to slob about.'

'Am I my brother's keeper?' I asked.

We drank our coffee in silence, not companionable.

*

Our church has a beach mission every year, middle two weeks in August.

You know the sort of thing, big tent, band, community singing, balloons for the children, sermons. People seem to enjoy it but then they'll enjoy anything on a summer's day when the sun is shining and there's just sufficient breeze (4 mph) to keep the midgies at bay. Oh, I remember the great glory days when there were five tents, and a full rota of ten preachers and a choir of a hundred, and thousands upon thousands of people listening.

Ours is a bit more modest these days. Just the one tent, and me with my portable keyboard, and three or four people from the choir leading the singing.

But when conditions are right, the people flock.

Sometimes they mock, but Peter could deal with that.

Looked at them earnestly and asked what do you mean?

And I support him with Onward Christian Soldiers, full blast.

Our theme this year was Love One Another.

It wasn't until about the fifth day I began to wonder if something was wrong. I was busy with all the background organisation of it, which they always leave to me, for I am good at it. And with that and the organ I wasn't really listening to Peter's sermons.

My sister always wrote his sermons, from the early days of their marriage. She had a natural bent in that direction, being a great reader with a very analytical mind. As a result his sermons were noted for their spiritual depth and theological rigour, and frankly, that is what the members of our church liked. Peter with his serious demeanour was well suited to this style of preaching.

After she died, he continued to recycle the old sermons, on the principle that what was worth hearing once was worth hearing again. He sometimes did it while she was alive, if there was a week when she was out of sorts.

But here at the beach mission this year something had changed.

What he was preaching was psychobabble. That is the only word I could use to describe it. Shallow selfhelpspeak, bitty, incoherent, the sort of thing I've heard you get on afternoon television. Not at all our style. Where was he getting this?

I had my suspicions. I didn't say anything. I watched and listened.

As the days went by, Peter became jumpier. He kept losing the sense of what he was saying, not surprising, since a lot of it made no sense. He would pause, as if he knew that, and eye Heather warily, but she sat smug on her canvas folding chair and smiled at him encouragingly.

Altogether it was a somewhat uneasy mission.

On the last morning we were beginning to wind down. At our tea break we normally just have digestive biscuits, but today I had brought a tin of my home made scones which I handed round, some with butter, some with jam, some with butter and jam. Different people have different tastes. When I came to Heather, she glanced in the tin and smirked and shook her head. Solid stodge, she murmured to no one in particular.

I offered the tin to Peter. He hesitated and then took one. Butter and jam, which he likes.

'Peter, your diet,' Heather said.

He looked at the scone, from which he'd taken a bite, and gave his silly little laugh.

'Well,' he said.

'Well what?' I answered.

The two of us watched him eat it. That woman had spoiled his enjoyment of it, it was as ashes in his mouth, but he ate it, throwing the last crumbs to some waiting seagulls.

Then he gave the signal to start again, and we went on with the mission.

His sermon that day had a new theme.

He preached on the need for each one of us to find a quiet corner and be by ourselves and alone.

What are we, he appealed to us, if constantly surrounded by other people, pressured, burdened, we cannot sink down into ourselves and find our own truths, deep in our souls, *alone*. He made a fervent plea for us each to find our own wilderness. He finished to mild applause.

As I played the intro for the last hymn, All Things Bright and Beautiful, I caught a glimpse of Heather's face. It was set in annoyance.

Then it was all over. The mission tent had to be dismantled and everything tidied up. Everyone took a bin bag and gathered up the rubbish round about.

'Peter?' I said, casually. 'Who wrote that sermon for you?'

'I wrote it myself,' he said.

'Really,' I said. 'Who wrote the rubbish you've been using all week?'

'I did,' said Heather behind me.

I turned and stared at her. 'I have never presumed,' I said. 'To interfere with the Word. While she was alive my sister wrote his sermons. I know better than to try and improve on them.'

'Oh, those old things. They belong in the ark. What's needed is a new approach.'

'And do you think that was it?' I turned to Peter. 'You should be ashamed of yourself, lending yourself to such travesties.'

'Peter, you agree they're much better,' said Heather.

'They are not,' I said. 'Peter, it was a mistake, you'll acknowledge.'

'People like them,' said Heather.

'They do not.'

Peter started to cry.

Without warning he turned and walked to the edge of the sea and waded in.

A reporter from the local newspaper and his photographer, and a policeman, and several people left over from the mission stopped what they were doing to watch.

Go for it, man, somebody shouted.

I doubted if he could swim.

'He can't?'

By this time the water was over his head, and his location was marked only by the bin bag, which he was still clutching, filled with air and ballooning above him.

Heather stripped off all her clothes and ran, naked, into the sea. She grabbed hold of him by the hair, and pulled him back to the shore.

She threw him onto the beach and gave him the kiss of life. The photographer was snapping away.

He coughed and spluttered and opened his eyes.

I said 'Really Peter, did you think you could walk on water?'

I was bending over him and wasn't quick enough. He hit me a blow that sent me reeling, and as I lay gasping, with the sky swooping and dipping overhead, I heard the reporter muttering MINISTER ASSAULTS ORGANIST.

The photographer took some more pictures.

So those are the events that led to the charges against Peter. He's to appear before a hearing of the church authorities and explain himself, charged with bringing the church into disrepute, and conduct unbecoming etc. Possibly not the last one, that's the army. Sufficient to say he could be defrocked if found guilty.

I'll be keeping an eye.

Happy Families

I was sitting on the roof when this police car drove up and two policemen dragged me down and took me to the station. It was all right because the sergeant there knows me and knew it had just been a misunderstanding. He let me sleep in one of the cells since I couldn't be bothered walking all the way back to my digs. I'd like to know who it was phoned the police anyway. I asked the wife the next day and she said it wasn't her, because she hadn't noticed I was sitting on the roof. It must have been one of the neighbours who hadn't recognised me and thought I was a burglar. I thought it was a cheek myself because if a man can't sit on the roof of the house that is really his, even though the lawyer and the council made him, that is to say me, sign it over to my wife, without some interfering neighbour sending for the police then it's not a free country any more, that's all I can say.

I was there because I was wanting to speak to my wife's new husband as I had a business proposition to put to him. I was willing to overlook the unseemly haste with which she had encumbered herself with him because they are all at it now. They write a wee letter to the judge telling a lot of lies about their husband and the judge writes back and says all right, hen, you're divorced and the next day they belt down to the registry office and get themselves a new one. It's not the sort of thing you find a man doing. I said that to my wife when I went to see her and her new man with a crystal decanter which I gave them for a wedding present.

It doesn't matter what the judge said, I told her, if I was a catholic you'd still be married to me. It wouldn't matter whether you were a catholic or not she said I wouldn't still be married to you for anything and anyway it only counts if it's me that is the catholic. Exactly I said. That's the trouble

142

with women. They will argue with you but they have no sense of logic and can't follow through a reasoned discussion. Her new man just sat and didn't say anything. I had taken the precaution of filling the decanter with half a bottle of whisky because I knew my wife would be unlikely to have anything in as she is dead against drink, and we all had a glass or two. At least her new husband only had one and he sat and held it as if it was going to bite him. I wasn't surprised because it turned out he worked in an office, which to my mind is only a suitable place for wee lassies to work in.

I told him about the time I was in Saudi Arabia and I could see he was impressed. I would still be there as a matter of fact if the manager hadn't had it in for me because I was so good at the job and he was afraid if he went on leave I would get his job and he would be told not to come back, which was very likely as he was the kind of manager who took spites against his good employees and didn't stand by his men when they were in trouble. Of course it was in his interests that I was deported but I am not saying it was him told the Arabs I had a few bottles on me. How they expect a man to work in that heat without a refreshment beats me. Of course, a man like my wife's new husband wouldn't understand that sort of thing, never having done anything more adventurous than sit behind a desk and write receipts.

I got a bit excited because telling them reminded me of the disgust I felt at the company at the time and I thumped the table to emphasize how unjust the whole thing had been, and unfortunately the decanter fell off the table and broke, which was a pity, but no great loss as I had finished the whisky that was in it. It wasn't really crystal anyway but just a glass one that I had picked up at the barrows.

To show there were no hard feelings because my wedding present had been broken I visited them regularly after that. I dropped in two or three times a week. It didn't matter if they were out because I still had a key to the front door so I could let myself in, and wait for them to come home. Sometimes they were awfully late and if they had been to the pictures they must have had a long romantic walk afterwards. I kidded them about it. How they could afford to go out so often I don't know. My wife used to argue with me all the time about going out when I was going down to the pub for a pint. She kept on about it, till you would think it was criminal, but now with her new man she was out gallivanting all the time.

When they were first married they didn't go out much, so they were always in when I went to see them. They sometimes had the television on and didn't hear me at the door, but if I had left the key on my other key ring I just banged and shouted till they heard me. Bet you weren't actually watching television, I used to say, doing something more interesting that you couldn't come to the door. Her new man got awfully red in the face. It was a laugh right enough to see him so embarrassed.

When I left the police station I went round to ask my wife why the key hadn't fitted the lock the previous night, but of course she explained that she had changed the locks because there had been burglaries in the street and she had lost her keys and she was scared the burglar would find them, so that was all right. I told her what I thought of the person who had reported me to the police for sitting on my own roof, and she asked me what I was doing on the roof anyway so I explained I was trying to get in and talk to her new husband. I was surprised they hadn't heard me, but she said they both slept sound.

Anyway, it wasn't worthwhile going back to my digs so I just stayed there all day until her husband came in from his work that night. He was very surprised to see me there, as well he might because he knows I am a busy man and haven't the time to hang about waiting for him.

While our wife gave us our tea I put it to him straight that he was wasting his time working in an office for peanuts when he could come into business with me. All it needed was a little bit of capital and unfortunately my capital was all tied up in sound investments for long term growth so if he could see his way to raising a hundred pounds to buy stock with we would be on our way and nothing to stop us becoming another Marks and Spencer. I could see he was very enthusiastic but the wife kept butting in and telling him to have nothing to do with it, which I thought was very unfair and shortsighted. After all, I said to her, she was the one that used to complain when I was between jobs and had no security, and here was I offering her new man a chance to become self-employed and independent. I would have told her just to shut her mouth, but I didn't because I reckoned it was not my place to do so, in the circumstances, and up to her new man.

I couldn't persuade him to invest any money right away so I invited both of them to the barrows the next Sunday to see my new business in operation.

As luck would have it, it was a foul day that Sunday, and I couldn't display the stock to its best advantage on account of having to keep it under cover. It did clear up a bit about ten o'clock so I spread the computers out on the board in front of the stall and started my spiel to attract the customers of which there were a few about, even in the rain.

I saw a boy with his dad and gave them the sales talk about this new micro-computer which was only £4.99 and a bargain at that, educational and would help the kid get his Highers. I was showing them how it worked when the wean stuck his fingers into it and god knows how he managed it but couldn't get his hand out again, for it was jammed in between the data bank recorder and the wee button you press to make the lights flash, and he was yelling blue murder. I said to his dad that in the circumstances I would only charge £3.99 and the man said he was damned if he would and it was only a bit of plastic anyway, so we started arguing. My wife and her new man chose that minute to turn up though I didn't see them right away on account of I had just punched the man for saying I was drunk which was a dirty lie. The punch only landed on his shoulder, which I did deliberately on account of not wanting to hurt him, but he started shouting that he was going to send for the police and charge me with assault. I said I would charge him with theft if his kid didn't give me back the computer terminal, and he wrenched it off the wean's hand and threw it at me. In the circumstances I considered it expedient to pretend the incident was over, and anyway it had started to rain again and all the merchandise was getting wet.

I was getting a bit fed up with the whole thing by this time because I had only sold a ceedee at twenty two pence, and the man in the pub that sold me the stall and told me it was a cushy number was a liar, that's the kindest thing I can say about him. Just then anyway the man that collects the rent for the barrows came round and said I had no right to be there on account of every stall needed permission when it changed hands which I hadn't got. He said he wouldn't have me within ten miles of the place, which I could not understand, but thinking about it now I suppose he was acquainted with the manager in Saudi Arabia and had been listening to lies about me.

I just walked away as it seemed the best thing to do, especially as the wife and her new man were standing watching.

I went round to see them that night. They didn't hear me at the door so I shouted to make them hear and just kept on banging. He must have been awfully deaf right enough. I know the wife doesn't know what's what and is so wrapped up in herself anyway she wouldn't notice if the moon fell down, but you would think with him working in an office he would be alert, but it took an awful lot of shouting to bring him to the door. He stood on the step and his mouth was opening and shutting, but I couldn't make out what he was saying because I was feeling a bit tired by this time, so I pushed past him and went into the house and lay down on the couch.

I supposed I must have fallen asleep because the next thing I knew I was in the ambulance on the way here, which was a surprise because I didn't know I was ill.

So here I am in this hospital where the nurses treat you quite well though one of the doctors has got hold of the wrong end of the stick and keeps saying I would be well if I gave up the whisky. He's black and doesn't understand what whisky is on account of they don't have it where he comes from. I just agree with him because it seems a shame not to and it makes him that pleased.

I was hearing, actually, just the other day that the wife's new man is away from her, and that suits me fine, because I have decided to leave here and go back and live with her. Whether we get married again or not I will make up my mind about depending on how she behaves herself. I'll be leaving here any day now, but I won't let her know I'm coming. I'll just arrive.

Lentils

Agnes was making soup with insect repellent.

She had tried other things, hair spray, perfume, rat poison, bath cleaner, aftershave. She had hopes of the last one, thinking Edgar wouldn't notice the smell since he was always smothered in it anyway, but the taste was foul.

She found the midgie spray was best by accident in the garden one day, getting some onto her fingers which she licked. It actually tasted not bad, slightly bitter, but no more than some of the medicine she'd been given as a child.

She tried just the tiniest drop in some lasagne and Edgar hadn't noticed, just commenting on the slight lemony smell it produced. He'd eat anything she put in front of him. It was one of the few things she'd been able to boast about to other women. Anything without complaint and probably compliment her on it, usually with a vague reference to starvation in the third world and be thankful. She sometimes tried cooking badly deliberately and found it produced the same reaction.

After eating the spiked lasagne he had an upset tummy all night. So far, so good.

The Church's Communal Soup Day had been thought up by Edgar and was now an eighteen year old tradition. He preached the same sermon every Sunday before it, the gist being the advancement of mankind from primeval stew to communal soup. She sat in the manse pew gritting her teeth. The village, as far as she was concerned, was a cauldron of seething sludge.

For the big day all the women in the church contributed a couple of litres of home made soup. Lentil had been decided as being the easiest and cheapest, and least likely to provoke competition, but naturally most of them added a little touch of their own, some garlic here, some sage there, sweetcorn,

148

peppers, and now Agnes measured out her generous helping of poison. All the soup would be mixed together in one big pot in the church hall, and reheated. The whole village came.

She hummed as she stirred.

There would be no more listening to other women tell her how nice Edgar was. She would scream if one more person said it to her. Nice! Nice! He was a poultice, a wet deadweight. Not like Daddy. Daddy was the right kind of minister. When he wasn't out visiting, he was in his study writing his sermon, which generally took him the entire week. Mummy had been able to be a real minister's wife. She ran the Womens Guild and the Sunday school, the Band of Hope, the Tea Meeting, the Prayer Guild and the Missionary Society. They had clearly defined roles that satisfied everybody. They never saw Daddy, except in the pulpit on Sundays.

Edgar was a modern minister, a new man, round her feet all the time, chattering about counselling and empowerment, organising the flower rota and the healing group, and just about everything else. The minister should do the minister's work, not the work of his wife. It came, she knew, from him having less to do, what with short pithy sermons that could be written on a postcard, and not enough people to visit, but it was unfair that she should be denied the authority Mummy had.

Dear Mummy. Maybe they could live together. Mummy was still a power to be reckoned with in her church, even though Daddy was long gone.

'You in your small corner

And me in mine...' sang Agnes as she crumbed the mixture for the scones, for of course soup didn't mean literally just soup.

The soup simmered gently.

It was, she reckoned, a work of art, a scientific marvel, a dream of a soup, an exquisitely calculated mathematical

149

exercise. She had measured her ingredients carefully. It was fairly concentrated so that when it was added to the big pot with everyone else's soup in the church kitchen it would make people just a little bit ill. Not all of them perhaps, for some had stronger stomachs than others. Then when Edgar died after being fed some more of the insect repellant, probably in scrambled egg, that was his favourite, they would assume he had just reacted worse than the others.

She pictured him vomiting over the lavatory pan and smiled.

And when they investigated, they would assume it had got into the pot by accident. They would never be able to trace who or how.

Aren't I the cleverest girl, she thought.

There was the sound of a car outside. The doorbell rang. Agnes opened the door to a man in a suit and a very sinister smile, with a younger man behind him.

'Is the reverend at home?'

'No, I'm his wife. Can I help?'

'Environmental Health.' He showed her his identification card, which she scrutinised carefully. She always wanted in such circumstances to say the photo doesn't look at all like you, sorry, I don't believe you're who you say you are, go away, but she never did.

'Come in.'

Once in the kitchen he explained. 'There's been so much poisoning you see. Food poisoning. The regulations have been tightened up. So you can only sell food that's been cooked on the premises. In the church in other words. And of course the kitchens have to come up to standard. I'm very sorry, but it means you can't hold the soup day tomorrow, not the way you've been doing it in the past.'

'But we're all ready for it. Everyone's done the cooking.'

'I'm sure the soup's very wholesome.' He sniffed. 'Smells good. But regulations are regulations.'

The back door opened.

'Mother,' cried Agnes.

'Hullo dear I thought I'd surprise you. I've brought something for your soup day.' She put a package on the table. The smell of home made bread filled the kitchen.

There was another car outside.

'Dear God,' cried Agnes. 'Is the whole world coming to visit.'

Edgar bounced in accompanied by two of his elders.

Agnes burst into tears.

The environmental officer looked embarrassed. He repeated to Edgar what he'd already told Agnes. She saw them all watching her cautiously, Edgar, her mother, the two environmental health officers, the two elders. She rested her head on the table and wept.

'Overwrought,' said her mother. 'She always was prone.'

'Stress, a terrible modern scourge,' said Edgar. They all nodded. Hysteria was difficult, stress they understood.

'There, there my dear. It will be all right. We'll organise something.'

Agnes wailed.

'Tell you what. It's nearly one o'clock. Why don't you all stay for lunch? What do you say, Agnes. It's a shame to waste your good soup. It's ready, isn't it, and mother's bread too, thank you mother. Come gentlemen, it's lentil, we won't take no for an answer. It just needs bringing through the boil again. That's right my dear, you go and lie down. We'll have a talk later. Mmm smells delicious. Agnes always has a secret ingredient. Smells sort of citrusy. Lemon, Orange perhaps? Sit in, everyone. Mother, dear, will you say grace?'

Agnes quietly closed the door behind her.

Occupational Therapy

'A greenhouse is like a womb,' said Henry.

'Now, now,' said the nurse. 'We'll have none of that kind of talk.' She pushed Elsie forward. 'I'll leave you for an hour, Elsie,' she said. 'I'll come back for you at half past three.'

'I haven't a watch,' said Elsie.

'It doesn't matter. You stay here till I come for you.'

She left. Elsie closed the door behind her. Loose panes rattled gently.

The impression was of size, and light, brighter than the grey day outside, and not the clamminess she had expected, but dry and pleasantly warm.

The staging held rows of pot plants, some of which she knew to be geraniums. Under the eaves massed tomato plants grew out of the earth, their bunches of fruit beginning to redden. It all stretched away from her to the far gable like the art teacher's perennial lesson in perspective, only he, so many years ago, had used a battlefield of rearing horses and fallen bloody lances.

Henry was watching her, while his fingers tamped earth into a flower pot.

'You know about greenhouses, do you?' he asked.

'My grandfather had one.'

She had chosen the greenhouse because she thought it would be quiet. Despite their promises, the hospital wasn't peaceful. There were too many people. When she didn't answer the nurses, they reported her to the doctor and he came and made her talk about why she didn't want to talk. He'd made her discuss her grandfather's greenhouse. Somehow, it wasn't altogether clear to her how, she had pleased him, though it upset her, dragging out of remote memories still more detail for him to analyse and add to her

152

deadweight of self-knowledge. The doctor called it a useful session and had approved of her doing occupational therapy in the hospital's greenhouse.

'Been here long?' asked Henry.

'Oh, weeks. Going home soon.'

She looked round again. There was no one in the place except her and Henry.

'Most women do knitting,' he said.

'They let me choose anything.'

He shrugged. 'All one to me. Only, women usually do knitting.'

He heaved a bag of potting compost onto the bench and slit it open with his thumbnail. He showed her how to lift the compost in handfuls into a seed tray, breaking up the lumps, patting it firm. She copied his movements, liking the dry peaty feel of the stuff.

Crumble, spread, pat. They worked in silence, save for an occasional word of apology when their hands knocked each other as they lifted the soil from the bag. Elsie relaxed. She glanced at Henry for his approval and he nodded to her.

Lift, crumble, pat. One seed tray. Two seed trays. Three. As she filled each one he took it from her and added it to the row, and gave her an empty one.

Crumble, spread, pat.

Her new summer dress was white with pink commas printed on it. They had bought her a pink cardigan to go with it. She read once, long ago, that well-dressed women didn't need cardigans. They were for children and old ladies. But it seemed to her if she protested about the cardigan that might cause another talk with the doctor and today she felt she couldn't face that, so she was wearing it.

Her feet felt clumsy in her outdoor shoes. She had worn slippers for the last six weeks.

'The theory of a hot-house,' said Henry, 'is to provide a protective, nurturing environment where growth may take place without stress. It is no coincidence that psychiatric hospitals such as our own have a greenhouse as part of the occupational therapy programme. The atmosphere of warmth and quiet is conducive to rehabilitation.',

She finished filling a tray and waited for him to take it, but he ignored her.

'Namely,' he continued. 'Womb-like.'

'Well,' said Elsie. 'I thought it would be nice and quiet.'

'In due course of time,' he went on, 'plants, and people, can be gradually hardened off, ready to be exposed to the outside world. The outside world is a cold place.'

In the yoga class they had to imagine they were a rose, opening up to the rays of the sun. Elsie was very good at it, so good that when it came to the second part of the exercise, closing their petals up again as the sun goes down, Elsie told the teacher her petals were brown and withered and scattered on the ground and therefore could not be closed up again. That had given the doctor something to analyse at their next session.

She watched Henry uncoil a hosepipe and lay it along the floor. Water trickled from the nozzle, which he picked up and adjusted, till water came out in a fine spray over the seed trays they had been filling.

He turned slightly and some of the water splashed over Elsie. She stepped back.

'Watch what you're doing.'

He put the hosepipe down, closing off the water. 'Are you all wet?'

'Of course I'm wet. That was stupid.'

He reached out his hand and plucked at her sleeve. 'Best take it off. You'll get cold.'

'No, it's all right,' she said, trying to shake his hand off.

'Come on, take it off.' He tightened his grip, and now his fingers were digging into her arm. He turned and began pulling her to the far end of the greenhouse.

'There's a stove up here. We'll soon have it dry.'

She looked back over her shoulder. The door was growing smaller and smaller in the distance, the perspective swinging round, blocking off her escape. She stumbled, her feet clumsy in their heavy shoes. Henry's hand was hurting her.

'Let me go,' she cried.

The stove stood in a corner of the greenhouse, surrounded by paraphernalia of a man's howff, a dirty wooden chair, a stool which had once been a chair, muddy outdoor shoes tucked under the stove, drying. There was a cardboard box filled with gardening magazines. There was a tin box filled with coal and some logs beside it. There was a cupboard with double doors, the top piled with sprays and cartons and balls of twine. A blackened teapot steamed gently on top of the stove.

Elsie sat down in the chair, relieved that at least Henry had stopped touching her. She watched him as he opened the cupboard and pulled out a packet of tea. He scrabbled in it, drawing out a large handful of tea-leaves which he dropped into the teapot. He threw a piece of coal into the stove and kicked the door shut.

Elsie picked up a gardening magazine from the box beside her. This uncovered a naked woman smiling up at her from a copy of Playboy. Blushing, she dropped the gardening magazine. Henry was busying himself with mugs.

The tea was very strong, and without asking her he topped up both mugs with condensed milk poured from the tin.

'You can hang your cardigan over the line.' He indicated a rope strung above the stove. 'It'll dry in no time.'

She took off her cardigan and handed it to him. He untied one end of the rope and threaded it through, first one sleeve, then across the back and down the other sleeve, and hooked the rope up again.

The cardigan hung there, sleeves outstretched, like a pink feminine crucifixion, till Elsie could bear it no longer and rose and unhooked the line.

She slid the cardigan off and retied the rope and folded the cardigan over it neatly, looping up the sleeves close to the body so it no longer looked alive.

She sat down again, relieved, and sipped her tea. She pointed to the cupboard, the door of which Henry had left open. 'You read a lot?'

He reached in, pulled out some of the books and handed them to her. She read the titles.

Psychology for Everyman.

An Introduction to Psychoanalysis.

The Role of the Psychiatrist in a Modern Industrial Society.

'You have to keep up to date in this business,' said Henry. 'Theories keep changing.' He took the books from her and returned them to the cupboard beside the others.

'I'm going home in a few days,' said Elsie. 'I've got better.'

She saw now that he wasn't as old as she'd first thought. There was very little grey in his thinning hair, and what she had mistaken for wrinkles round his eyes were merely whiter flecks of skin, as if he spent a lot of time outside screwing up his eyes against the sun. His hands were blackened. She glanced at her cardigan, making out the darker patches of dirt.

'Someone coming,' he said.

Since Elsie had come into the greenhouse it had started to rain, a fine shower which distorted the glass without obscuring it. They could see a woman walking up the path which led from the side gate to the main block of the hospital. Despite the mild weather, she wore a fur coat, but no hat, and her hair was frizzed with a halo of moisture. Her progress was jerky, for the path was only compacted earth stepped with old railway sleepers, and the woman was wearing stiletto heels. She paused occasionally. Elsie had seen her before. She came regularly to visit her husband, who did not know her.

As they watched, there was a flurry of movement among the trees above the walker, and down the path there ran a woman in a summer dress, wearing bedroom slippers. She was crying. The woman in the fur coat spoke to her, but she shook her head, and plunged on down the path, disappearing from the view of the watchers in the greenhouse. The woman in the fur coat looked after her a moment, then turned and walked on until she too was out of sight.

Elsie's cardigan swung gently in the rising heat.

'Know anything about flowers?'

'I had a badge for wild flowers in the Guides,' she said. 'Only I didn't really.' She was fluent in the telling, for this was one of the things she'd already told the doctor. 'I was in the Guides. You got badges for all sorts of things. Cooking. Sewing. Map reading. Swimming. Anything you were good at. You sewed them onto your sleeve. One girl had them going up both sleeves. I just had the one you get for being in a year. One day the patrol leader gave me a book about wild flowers and told me to write about them. It was all laid out, a flower to a page, description, habitat, everything. I copied out about a dozen of them and put it into proper sentences, and handed it in. And they gave me a badge. I had to step out of the circle before Taps to collect it. I left the Guides after that.'

'What for? You'd got your badge.'

'They must have known. It was all in the same order as in the book. Nobody asked me any questions. They must have known I was a fraud.'

She began to cry.

'Nerves,' said Henry. He reached into the back of the cupboard and pulled out a shoe box. It was full to the brim

157

with bottles of pills, bottles of capsules, foil sheets of tablets, ampoules of liquid. He rummaged through it.

'What are you on? I've got most of them here. Xanax, Mianserin, Mogadon, Oxazepam. Name your poison.' He knelt down in front of the cupboard and reached into the bottom of it. 'I've got some amphetamines here.' He pulled out a tin which had once contained Quality Street and eased off the lid to reveal it half full of loose pills, multi-coloured. He selected a blue one and offered it to her. 'Go on. Do you good.'

'I'm nearly better,' she said. 'I'll be going home soon.'

He shrugged. 'Suit yourself.' He dropped the pill back in the tin and returned it to the back of the cupboard.

She put down her mug on the floor and reached up for her cardigan. He was on his feet too, taking it from her, and then he was holding it open for her to put it on.

She turned her back on him and eased one arm into the sleeve. As she did so, his hand closed over her right breast and squeezed. She leapt away from him, banging her hip on the staging, one arm tangled in her cardigan, the other flailing at him.

'Aw come on,' he said. He caught her hand and pulled her towards him.

'I'll tell them,' she sobbed.

'Who'd believe you?' He laughed. 'Tell me, who would believe you?'

The loose panes rattled gently as the nurse pushed open the door.

On the way back to the main building the nurse asked, 'Are you going again on Thursday?'

Elsie shook her head.

'No,' said the nurse. 'Dirty kind of work, really. We'll try something different. Raffia maybe. Or embroidery. Embroidery's nice.'

Deadly Routine

I enjoy my work. I practically had to beg for the job. They didn't believe someone who'd taken early retirement from being a bank manageress would want a job clearing tables in an airport cafeteria.

It's because I was a manageress, thirty two people working under me, that I wanted the job, I told them. Just physical work, no responsibility, go home at night and no worries. I suppose I could have lied, and pretended I was just a cleaner at the bank, but why lie when the truth doesn't hurt?

I like it. I have fifteen tables to attend to, and a workstation in the middle where I stack the dirties and empty the slops. I do the job with the same care I gave to the bank. I like the way a mess of a table can be restored, quickly, half a dozen movements, neat, contained, lift the dishes onto the tray, condiments to the chair, spray the disinfectant, wipe with the cloth, return the condiments clean and dry, the salt and pepper and sugar bowl awaiting the next customer. It is a matter of pride to me that no one ever has to wait for a table to be cleared, not in my section. The instant people are moving away from the table, I'm there, preparing it for the next customer.

After all if you're leaving on a journey, the last thing you want is a table looking like a Regent Street pavement after a Saturday night.

But don't misunderstand me, please. I don't relate to any of the customers. They collect what they want at the line, bring it to the table, eat it, and leave. They're passing through, flying out to everywhere in the world and already mentally in the air and on their way. They don't look at me and I don't look at them. Nobody ever looks at a cleaning woman. It suits me.

And I lost six kilograms in the first six weeks.

Banking of course had its own excitements, especially dealing with people looking for loans, the things you could find out. If you wanted power you could have it, but here it's different. Here it is standing on the sidelines watching what's going on. Stacking and wiping and sweeping, you see a lot. I saw a man who was a customer of the bank, lives a couple of streets away from me, having coffee with a girl who wasn't his wife. She was crying. They weren't flying anywhere, not then, probably not ever from the looks of it, just using the place for a quiet invisible talk. I kept out of his line of sight, but even if he'd seen me, so what, he wouldn't have recognised me, a middle aged woman in a green overall. Fine chance for some blackmail, but my line isn't blackmail, so forget it.

The number of times I've seen drugs being passed. In fact one crowd had it off pat. To the security cameras it would look like a family party, giving garishly wrapped presents brought back from abroad, laughing and pushing the kids around. I had to admire them. If you're going to break the law, do it boldly and openly and nobody will notice. I noticed, because I saw the same couple several times, subtly different each time, meeting different people, different children in tow for cover. Sometimes they looked like they were giving farewell gifts to people going abroad, but who's to say where they went when they left the cafeteria.

Fooled other people, maybe. Fooled security, maybe. But not me.

But of course it was none of my business.

I first saw the man I was interested in on a Friday afternoon in early May. He looked like an ordinary businessman flying out, and for all I know that was what he was. It was easy to establish that it was Paris he was going to. He sat at a corner table, close to a monitor, and kept glancing at it. When his flight was signalled, he picked up his briefcase and left. I watch the monitor too.

160

He turned up regularly, always on a Friday. Not every Friday, maybe one in three, sometimes a gap and then two Fridays in succession. Habitual travellers like the routine of their usual table, as an insulation from the crowds. He was a man like that. He would collect a coffee from the line, and use the same table or one nearby if his usual one was full. It was usually the table for two in the corner, where there isn't much passing traffic. A sweet tooth too, always three or four sachets of sugar from the bowl in front of him. When the 3 o'clock Paris flight was signalled he would get up and go, leaving his newspaper which I would tidy away.

In between Fridays I carried a clear picture of him in my head. He was losing his hair, which might once have been blond but was now colourless, neither blond nor gray. He wasn't good looking. His face was too thin for that, with lines and loose skin round his jawline, as if he had once been fatter and lost weight but the skin hadn't shrunk to match. But a nice face. He had brown eyes and a sweet mouth. Once I was clearing his table when he arrived and he thanked me, just a couple of words but enough for me to catch the Irish in it. My pleasure I said, making my voice warm, and willing him to make eye contact which was bad of me, but I really couldn't resist it. He glanced at me, and smiled automatically in response to mine. He smelled of Brut. I imagined him working out at a gym after lunch, and showering and changing into his business suit and driving to the airport and by dinner time he would be in Paris.

I never saw him return, but then he wouldn't want to use the cafeteria, would just want to get home.

We work shifts in the job. Whoever works Fridays has to do the weekend as well, so some people don't like it. That's no problem for me, so the other workers would swop. That way I made sure I was always there on a Friday.

Sometimes I didn't go near his table when he was there. Sometimes I would have liked to but didn't get the chance. My tables became hectic as the summer came in, and with

161

the school holidays there were more children, and more noise and more mess. But I always knew when he was there.

I only spoke to him once more, after that first time. The second time was on the day he died.

I saw him in the line collecting his coffee and went over and cleared the table in the corner. A honeymoon couple were just leaving, and I cleared away her cup with its lipstick stains and his, which had hardly been touched and had slopped in the saucer. I wiped the table and lifted off the sugar bowl and put down one I had prepared earlier. He was there by that time.

People *will* play with the sugar, I said.

He put his coffee down and sank into the chair. Thank you, he said.

My pleasure.

He smiled but didn't look at me. It was only a reflex. There was no connection.

From my work station I watched him tear open the sachets, four, and sugar his coffee and drink it in slow sips, with the newspaper open in front of him, absorbed in what he was reading.

When he left I gathered up the newspaper and lifted the sugar bowl, replaced it with the original one, and took my stacked tray over to my work station, where I disposed of his detritus along with everybody else's.

It was in the news that evening that a passenger had been taken ill and died on the 3 p.m. flight to Paris. They didn't give the name, but the age sounded right, and I never saw him again.

The police came round looking for the source of the poison. I pity whoever had to sit through dozens of security cameras worth of film to trace his steps from the car park to the cafeteria, to the gents perhaps, then out to the concourse, and onto the plane. And what did the film of the cafeteria show? Me doing my job.

When I was a bank manager I knew the inside out of everybody's lives, for when you know someone's finances you know a lot about them. I find I don't want to know about people now. What he did for a living, or in what way he annoyed the organisation is no concern of mine. They can be assured of my absolute discretion, based on a total lack of interest.

The money the organisation has paid into my bank account is very satisfactory indeed. I hope I can be of use to them in the future. But I'll go on working in the airport cafeteria for a while yet, so I don't draw attention to any change in my routine. Besides, I like the job. It's very satisfying.

The Sister's Story

They told me I was lucky to have survived, but how many times have I wished that I had not.

Was Lazarus pleased to be snatched from the tomb? He was destined to die a second time, and his sisters, who had mourned him once, would have to mourn him again.

Philadelphia is a good place to live. But sometimes in the hot and humid summers or when the snow lies thick on the ground and travel is impossible, I think back to my home.

I loved the land of Galloway. I could show it to you on the map, at the end of Scotland where the air is mild, and the wind blows fresh in from the sea and sends the clouds tumbling across the sky. The harbours were always busy with ships from Holland and Spain and France. Some came from the Indies.

When my father went to market in Wigtown he took us in his cart, and I would plague my sister Maggie to take me down the hill to the harbour where she held tight to my hand in case I went too near the water. We watched the ships unloading wonderful things like silk cloth and wine, and the air would be full of the scent of spices.

My father's farm was prosperous then. We didn't have silks or spices, for these were for the gentry, but I had a blue bowl which came from a place called Delft. I used to have my porridge from it, and in the schoolroom I could trace the outline of Holland on the globe, and boast to the other girls about my bowl.

Forgive an old woman, crying over a piece of pottery, long ago broken to shards in the midden.

When I was old enough, Maggie took me to the meetings for worship in the quiet hidden places, where people met to sing and listen to the bible being read. Often these conventicles were led by old Sammy, who the rest of the week was the ploughman on the farm marching with ours, but on Sundays preached the word of God.

Walking home from these the women would tell me of how their grandfathers had signed the Covenant against the King who claimed he was head of the church. He wanted us to have bishops and use the English prayer book. Christ is head of the church, not any king. They told me of how all the ministers had left their churches rather than submit to the King's will. That King had died, killed by his own English subjects, and there was peace for a while when there was no King, but now his son, who was the new King, wanted to impose bishops again.

'Why must we have a King?' was one of the questions that I would ask, but no one could answer me.

But there were men who thought the same.

I lay curled up in my cot watching the flickering flames of the fire, and listened to my big brothers arguing with my father, far into the night.

'We were better when we had no King. He has no right to tell us how to worship.'

'This King signed the Covenant too.'

'Aye, and broke his word.'

'Better without.'

'Keep your head down,' said my father. 'If the King says kneel in the kirk then I kneel, if he says we have bishops then I'll bow to the bishops, if it means I keep a roof over my head and food in the bellies of my family.'

My three oldest brothers left home and went to Ireland. It was as well they went when they did. Soldiers came, who had orders to shoot anyone who would not say 'God Save the King'. My father and mother would readily say it. I was too little for anyone to ask me.

We played a game, my brother Tom and I. Tom was only two years older than me. I had a doll which my mother made, from scraps of cloth and sheepswool. We sprinkled water from the burn over it and named it the King. This made it our enemy, and Tom took the hatchet my mother used for killing the geese. I laid down the doll on the grass and Tom chopped off its head.

'Death to King Charles. Death to King Charles,' we chanted.

My father caught us, and whipped us both.

He forbade me from attending the field meetings, but Maggie went, even after it became treason, and they had to post lookouts to warn if soldiers were coming. My father whipped her, but he couldn't stop her.

My mother wept at night, and my father went around grim faced and would not speak to her. But Maggie was stubborn, and Tom stopped attending the kirk too, and went with her to the meetings.

James Calhoun was the minister of our parish. He was a good man, I think. He rode round all the people, and told us a new law had come that he had to send in a list of everyone who did not attend the kirk on Sundays. He tried to persuade everyone to come and take communion, even if only once, so that he did not need to put their names on the list.

My father and mother went. Maggie would not, and neither would Tom, and I clung to Maggie and said I would not go either. They could not force me. Mr Calhoun had to mark us on his list. He wrote Withdrawers after our names, meaning we had withdrawn from public worship. I was twelve years old.

They sent soldiers after that to seek out the people they called the rebels. In October of that year everyone who refused to swear the oath denouncing the Covenanters was made to appear at a special court in Wigtown. Three women refused to give evidence against their husbands. They were sentenced to be shipped to the colonies as slaves.

My father was also brought before the court and fined for the behaviour of his children. Soldiers came and searched the farm for hidden Covenanters. They stole some of my mother's pots, and trampled her kaleyard.

My father told Tom and Maggie they would have to leave home.

They talked about it long into the night.

'What about the bairn?' asked my mother.

I was curled up in a corner, listening to this.

'Nessie shall go too,' said my father.

Perhaps he was frightened if I stayed I would do or say something that would cause trouble for him, for I was but a child, and perhaps did not properly understand what was dangerous and what was not.

Did I understand? I understood as a child understands. I believed what Maggie believed for she was the person I loved most in all the world.

We left home and travelled into the mountains with others of like mind. We had cousins in Nithsdale and they hid us for as long as they could, and there were always cottars and shepherds who would find a corner for us to sleep in, and give us food. Most of the people were Covenanters. Even those who conformed and attended the kirk had some sympathy, for there was resentment against a king who wanted to impose his will, without the consent of our parliament or the people.

We attended conventicles in the hills, where we worshipped in our own way with no man to intercede between us and God and in truth in a bright summer dawn on a high moor with the whaups singing, it was a glorious adventure.

We had word sometimes of my father and mother. They had soldiers billeted on them, the soldiers who were given the work of hunting us and our kind out, for we were now called traitors.

Then in early March word came that King Charles was dead, and his brother James was to be the new King. There would be freedom for every person in the country to worship how they would. We rejoiced, because we thought our troubles were at an end.

Maggie and I went home, for we wanted to see our father and mother again. Tom would not come. He said he did not trust the rumours.

But when we reached the farm, we found soldiers there, and we daren't go in.

We hid, and when my mother came out to shut up the hens for the night she found us, and we all cried and embraced.

When everything was quiet, we left there and walked to Kirkinner. It was a starry night and everything was still, save for the cry of the owls. We walked quietly, not speaking, glad to be back in our own country. From the high ground I could see the sea glimmering and the hills beyond.

The dawn was breaking when we arrived at Mrs Maclachlan's cottage. We had not seen her for over a year. She was a widow. Her husband died for the cause, and she was known to be a kind help and supporter to all, a staunch worshipper at the conventicles, and frightened of no one. I don't know by what means she avoided the persecution that others suffered.

We tapped on her window at the back and she let us in. We talked, and she fed us, and we slept.

But we had been seen.

Later in the morning there was a knock on the door. Mrs. Maclachlan opened it and Patrick Stuart entered.

I did not like Patrick Stuart. I did not like the way he talked to Maggie sometimes when we were in Wigtown, nor the way he looked at her.

He was looking at her like that now, scornful and greedy at the same time. He sat down, though he was not invited.

'Ale, mistress,' he said.

Mrs. Maclachlan brought ale for him.

He lifted his cup, and proposed a toast to the King.

We were silent. He paused with his cup half way to his lips and looked at the three of us.

'God save the King,' he said again.

I looked at Maggie to see what she would do, for I was puzzled to know how to behave. But she shook her head gently.

'We toast no man,' she said.

'Come, come,' said Patrick. 'It is no ordinary man that I toast, it is the King. To the health of his Majesty, King James.'

Still Maggie sat and would not lift the cup to her lips. I did not either, though I was thirsty and longing for a drink, but I could not give a toast where it was wrong.

He drank the ale, and cursed and left the house.

We were walking home when we were stopped by a troop of soldiers on the road. One of them was Major Winram, who was in charge of all the soldiers in the area.

'I understand you refused to drink the health of the King,' he said.

'We drink the health of no man,' said Maggie, looking him straight in the eye.

We were taken to Wigtown and put down into the thieves hole in the tollbooth, as if we were common criminals.

They questioned us. They wanted to know the names and hiding places of other Covenanters. We didn't tell them, and for that I am proud to this day.

Mrs. Maclachlan was also arrested, and eventually they put all three of us in the same cell. She was a poor soul then, for they wouldn't allow us a fire or decent straw for a bed. This was in April and the place was still damp after winter rains. This didn't trouble Maggie or me, for we were young and strong, but Mrs. Maclachlan suffered greatly for she was old and troubled by rheumatism.

We were put on trial, the three of us, and three men who were also accused of being Covenanters. Our judges were

Major Winram, the Laird of Lagg, Colonel Graham who was the brother of Graham of Claverhouse, and the Provost and two councillors. These last three would not look at us. The Town Council had chosen earlier to renounce the Covenant, which they said was so that the town would be left in peace.

We were tried as traitors. We were accused of taking part in conventicles, which was against the law, and refusing to disclose the whereabouts of other Covenanters, which was treason. They said we were rebels and had been at the battles at Airds Moss and Bothwell Bridge, when Convenanters fought against the King's troops.

One of the men with us spoke up then.

'These lassies were but bairns when we fought at Airds Moss,' he said. He did not deny he had been there. The battle had been fought five years earlier. I was only eight years old and Maggie was thirteen and we were both of us living at home with our mother and father then. How could we have been at any rebellion?

'I saw them there,' said Major Winram. 'You,' he pointed at Maggie. 'Were whoring with the rebels.'

God surely punished him for his lies.

We were all found guilty. Mrs. Maclachlan and Maggie and I were to be drowned, which was the punishment for women who were traitors. The men were to be hanged. I did not cry in front of this court, but I cried later, back in the dungeon, while Maggie held me in her arms.

I don't know how many days we waited.

Then one day two soldiers came for me. They dragged me out of the cell. I screamed and struggled not because I thought I was going to my death, but because they were separating me from Maggie. She was screaming at them too, but they thrust her back into the cell.

I was taken outside the tollbooth and found my father there. He took my arm and hurried me away to where he had the horse and cart waiting to carry me back to the farm.

170

He told me he had travelled to Edinburgh, a hard ride that took many days, and pleaded for our lives. He swore a Bond for one hundred pounds and was given an authority to Major Winram that I was to be released because of my age and a promise that they would consider the matter of Maggie and Mrs. Maclachlan.

At home he locked me up in the attic room.

There were still soldiers billeted with us and my poor mother was at her wit's end to know how to feed them. Their horses ate all the oats which were intended for our own beasts.

On the day set for the punishment to be carried out I heard my father leave the house early. My mother and some of the neighbouring women were in the parlour, weeping and praying. I squeezed out through the window.

I ran all the way to Wigtown. It was the 11th day of May and I remember the smell of the broom and hawthorn, and skylarks singing.

There were others walking and some spoke to me, but I pulled my shawl over my head and kept running.

A couple riding in a cart stopped to give me a lift. They were strangers who didn't know me. I climbed into the back and sat atop their bundles. Their talk was of the executions. They were going to Wigtown in the hopes there would be crowds, and they would sell their goods, on which I was sitting.

When I understood this I was angry and shouted at them before jumping off when the horse paused at the ford.

I could see crowds at the harbour. As I ran down the hill I tripped and fell for I was now so thin that my gown trailed on the ground. I lay there sobbing till someone picked me up and carried me on.

The tide was full out, and ready to turn. There were already two stakes in the sand, out where the water would be deep.

It was very quiet when the soldiers brought the two women. Major Winram said to Mrs. Maclachlan and to Maggie 'Will you take the oath?' They both said no, they would not.

I saw my father push his way through the ranks of soldiers to Major Winram's side and seize his arm, ignoring the men who cocked their muskets at him.

'There is a pardon coming,' shouted my father. 'They promised me in Edinburgh. They are to be pardoned.'

Major Winram shook off his arm, and swore, and the soldiers came and dragged my father back.

The soldiers took Mrs. Maclachlan out to the furthest stake. They had almost to carry her, for she was weak from her imprisonment, and stiff in the limbs.

Then they brought Maggie. They tied her to the stake nearer the shore.

'She'll change her mind when she sees her fellow drown,' said a soldier near me.

The tide turns quickly on the Solway and comes in fast. As it lapped about the waist of Mrs. Maclachlan the soldiers standing beside her asked her would she renounce the Covenant. She shook her head.

I heard someone say 'The bairn' and some people took hold of me and tried to drag me back, out of sight of the shore, but I struggled and bit one of them on the hand and they let me go.

Major Winram was standing on the banking. The water was now up to Maggie's waist.

'Will you renounce the Covenant?' he shouted to her.

No.

He swore at her.

A groan went up from the people as the water closed over Mrs Maclachlan's head.

'What do you think of your friend now? She is in her death throes,' shouted Major Winram.

Maggie's voice came clearly.

'I see the struggles of Christ,' she answered.

When the water was up to her chest, Major Winram shouted at her again.

'Will you pray for the King?'

'I wish the salvation of all men, and the damnation of none,' was her answer.

My father cried out, 'Margaret, dear Margaret, say God save the King. Please Margaret, say God save the King.' Others took up the cry, and so did I. Please Margaret, say God Save the King.

She answered 'God save him, if he will.' Then she began singing a psalm, one of those we used to sing up in the hills.

The people on the shore shouted 'She said it, she said it', but Major Winram ignored them.

He said again. 'Will you renounce the Covenant?'

She didn't answer, but kept on singing. I think by now she was half crazed.

Then the water came up too far for the soldiers and they waded ashore. Soon the water was lapping against the quay, and everyone was silent. All I could see of Maggie was her hair floating on the surface like seaweed.

I was ill for a long time afterwards.

They let me alone. When I became stronger I helped my mother as best I could, but we had little to say to one another. I could never look my father in the face, for fear of what I would see there.

In time, the soldiers left. Everything was quiet, for the heart had gone out of the people.

There was now living at home just the four of us, my father, my mother, myself and my younger brother Gilbert, named for my father. What with the Bond my father had paid for my life and the burden of the soldiers and their horses, the farm was now so poor it could barely sustain us all alive.

So I came here to America, when this place was new, and settled among the Quakers. I did not much talk about my experiences, for many here had suffered worse. What had happened to me, save a few weeks in a prison cell?

They bring me word of another rising in Scotland. Another Charles who wants to be King. It matters naught here. I am glad to be in a country where the whim of an earthly king counts for nothing.

I have lived quietly. I have raised my children and they are a blessing to me. Soon I will join my man in the graveyard.

But, if truth be told, I think I died back there, on the shores of Wigtown Bay, with my sister.

Fergus and the Cost of Living

The media persisted in telling Fergus his pension was inadequate for him to live on. How could anyone have any life except poverty and degredation if they had such a miserable income?

What is life, he could have said, and frequently did, if we have no time to stand and stare, and he had plenty of that and it didn't cost anything?

But poverty, everywhere the words screamed at him. He must be living in cold misery, surely, if they were to be believed. And if you're not, you will be soon.

After a while he began to wonder if perhaps they were right. Could things only get worse?

He could sell some poems of course, but this would earn him no more than the money for a pint on a Friday night.

Perhaps the best thing would be to learn to live without money.

He pondered the ways open to him.

Che gelida manina, he sang as he dusted his bookshelves. To be a student, to live life in a garret. No responsibility, no cares, a thin gruel made with a hambone, a slice of stale bread, pool your resources with your friends and spend it in a glorious evening of wine and song.

And wasn't it true that hunger released the inspiration in the brain that led to great work? It was traditional, it was expected, it was almost compulsory, just like all great writers had to have a miserable childhood.

Fergus's childhood had not been particularly miserable, but it was a long way in the past.

Now, now was the time when he could mortify the flesh and produce his greatest work.

He would learn to live as the students do. He was already half way there. Didn't he lie in bed in the morning and write poetry?

His next door neighbour's son was a student. Fergus often saw him leaving the house, slouching, blue hair bespiked.

Fergus contrived a meeting at the bus stop and they travelled into the town together.

Fergus began his subtle search for information. What café would give a second coffee to a poor student and not charge for it?

Josh thought for a minute. Coffee in the ref was pretty cheap, half the price of elsewhere. Not that he drank coffee. He preferred hot chocolate.

The ref? The refectory. The student dining room.

Right. Then where did the students collect scraps from restaurant kitchens and share them with friends over a gas ring in their rooms, talking of poetry and music and the great philosophers?

Josh and his friends did their talking in the ref. The food there was good and cheap.

And what happened when the money ran out?

Well, Josh lived at home so there was no worry about that. His mum fed him. Most of his friends were the same. And there was the student loan if they needed money.

Yes of course. Did Josh not pine for a room of his own, for independent living, for freedom, for the life of Bohemia?

Not really. He was comfortable at home. He'd a job lined up in a bank in Birmingham so when he went there he'd be renting a flat till he could save a deposit to buy.

Fergus, saying goodbye, reflected that perhaps students were not what they were in his young day.

In the centre of town, he was accosted by a Big Issue salesman. Of course, here was poverty.

He gave the lad a pound, but declined the magazine.

Where did he go to eat when he had finished his stint? The Big Issue salesman pointed to the pizza joint behind him. Oh, just like anybody else?

I am just like anybody else, said the Big Issue salesman.

I was hoping, Fergus told him, to find somewhere, a soup kitchen perhaps where people who are hungry and have no money could find food, warmth, camaraderie.

The Big Issue salesman thought about this. There was the homeless mission over in the East End. You could eat there for next to nothing. So he'd heard. He'd never been there himself.

But aren't you homeless? Where do you sleep? Underneath the arches?

No, no, he had a room to himself in a hostel. Very nice and comfortable it was. A microwave and a kettle, though he hardly needed them, what with so many takeaways around. Yes, technically he was homeless.

Didn't Fergus want his magazine? He'd paid for it. The man wasn't a beggar you know. He was above that sort of thing, and it was a bit offensive for Fergus to treat him like a beggar when he wasn't. It was a sad day when uppity people could insult other people just because they were selling magazines on the street.

People were beginning to stare.

Fergus retreated rapidly along the street, with the Big Issue salesman shouting after him.

Although he'd had a good breakfast at home he'd walked it off and he easily persuaded himself into the frame of mind of a starving indigent.

He rehearsed the phrase to himself in his mind. A starving indigent. A tramp. A vagabond. A gentleman of the road. A wayfarer. A wanderer.

He was nearly in tears.

He made his way to the East End in search of the mission to the homeless. He had to ask a few times but eventually he stood outside a community centre.

Freedom's just another word for nothing left to lose, he sang to himself as he pushed open the door. He was greeted by a plump lady wearing spectacles who asked his name.

Welcome, Fergus, what would you like? There's food being served in the dining room if you would like to join us. He nodded. That was what he was here for.

The woman took him by the arm, which Fergus knew demonstrated her non-prejudicial attitude, or perhaps because she thought he might escape, and led the way through to the dining room. It was a large room and was filled with a lot of men and a few women at tables with seating for four. She led him to the serving hatch where a queue was waiting.

She read out the day's menu to him. There were three meat dishes and two vegetarian. One course was sixty eight pence, or he could have a full lunch for One pound fifty. Of course, if he had absolutely no money ...?

He assured her he could pay and chose a beef stew with potatoes, carrot and peas.

He took it to a table at which two men were already sitting.

Nice day, he said. They ignored him. They were ignoring each other too.

Nice place, he went on. My first time here. They did not answer, but went on eating.

Oh well, he thought, the camaraderie of the road wasn't working here. Perhaps, and the thought sneaked into his mind as he took a slice of bread from the piled platter on the table to mop up his gravy, perhaps they were too well fed. The food was excellent.

He examined them furtively. They were quite well dressed but not, he tried to frame the words carefully to himself, very clean.

He paused with his fork half way to his mouth and watched something walk along the corduroy shoulder of the

178

man sitting beside him. A tiny spider? A mite? A flea? The insect disappeared into a fold in the man's collar.

Fergus put down his utensils, coughed, and took a drink of water, and then casually pushed his chair back and crossed his legs, trying to make his action look spontaneous, as if wanting more leg room. The movement took him a bit further away from his companion.

When he left the table and returned his dirty plate to a trolley at the door, he was accosted again by the plump lady.

If he needed clothes. . . ? No, he didn't really need any clothes. What else might he need? A haircut? A doctor? Dental treatment? Training in computers? An outing. They were arranging a minibus next week for a visit to Alton Towers.

He looked round in despair. This wasn't at all what he wanted. Where were the absinthe drinkers, where the starving? Where were the gaunt philosophers, the poets, the artists?

There was a room where the artist in residence had his studio. If he wanted to paint he was welcome to use it.

Poetry? Oh, there was a creative writing group. They met on Thursday afternoons. Do come, she was sure he would enjoy it.

Fergus was gracious in his thanks. He would think about it.

He left and wandered out into the street.

He made his way through the city centre, jostled by the crowds. He was seeking he knew not what.

O wilderness!

He passed a beggar, sitting on the ground, polystyrene cup in hand, his faithful companion dog by his side, *Homeless and hungry, please help.* Was that what would become of him, when he became poor, when, as the media promised, his income would not be enough to live on.

Well, no. For one thing he didn't have a dog and could not imagine having one, for he was bitten by a chihuahua when he was a child and disliked them ever since. Not to say that he was frightened, of course he wasn't. But he wouldn't willingly go near a dog, especially not a small one.

And his rheumatism would trouble him if he sat on the ground. And he hadn't any ragged clothes.

He'd never taken drugs and his only drink was a few pints at the pub on a Friday night. And he wasn't exactly too old for free love but there wasn't the same urge as there might once have been.

Sadly, he did not qualify for the bohemian life.

Money wasn't everything. If you didn't think about money at all, then he had nothing to worry about. In fact he felt rich in many things.

He had his poetry. Suddenly he felt a poem coming on. He wandered blindly through the crowds spilling in and out of shops.

The first lines began to form in his head.

Homeless and hungry
Please help
In the midst of plenty
A sad gap

No, not gap. Space? Vacuum? He muttered the words aloud to get the rhythm of it. Lacuna? Lacuna was a good word. He'd just come across it recently. Yes, lacuna.

In the midst of plenty
A sad lacuna

There was a blare of horns and a hand grabbed at his arm and yanked him to one side

Feeling suicidal eh?

I was composing a poem, said Fergus with dignity.

Nonetheless he was grateful to his rescuer, who was brushing him down as if he had fallen to the ground, which of course he hadn't. A small crowd gathered.

You OK, pal?

Poor old man.

Away in a world of his own.

Could have been killed.

Has he got nobody to look after him?

The rescuer, a small man, continued to pat him on the shoulder, reassuringly. He looked more upset than Fergus felt. Someone pressed a pound coin into his hand.

The crowd dispersed cheerfully, grateful for the moment's entertainment.

The poem had gone from his head. He decided he'd had enough of the town. He wouldn't come here again. From now on he would be a recluse. He would turn his back on the world. It was the only way a poet could keep his dignity.

He made his way back along the street. He dropped the pound coin, now hot in his hand, into the cup of the young beggar with the dog.

Then he caught his bus home.

Snowdrops

The year they were married, Margaret's husband gave her a birthday posy of snowdrops which he gathered in the garden early in the morning. It became a ritual.

After her husband died Margaret invited her friends for tea every birthday. Each time she gathered snowdrops from her garden and tied them into bunches.

The friends were bound together with the threads of memories, confided griefs, love and exasperation. When they parted at the end of the afternoon each took a bunch of Margaret's snowdrops.

Each year the finicky tying of the thread took longer. The heads bending over the tea table were whiter. Each year there was one fewer bunch of snowdrops.

This year she picks only one bunch of snowdrops, and she does not trouble to bind it up with the white embroidery thread, for no one will be taking it out of its vase.

---o0o---

Lightning Source UK Ltd.
Milton Keynes UK
UKOW05f0331240614

233945UK00002B/9/P